MW01515355

the Thought of Romance

Legacy of the Heart

DANICA FAVORITE

3111201710911L0

Greene County Library
314 W. Main St
Paragould, AR 72450

2017

Copyright © 2017 by Danica Favorite

All rights reserved.

Cover design by Book Cover Bakery
Edited by Laurie Kuna
Formatted by Polgarus Studio

No part of this book may be reproduced in any form or by any electronic or mechanical means including information storage and retrieval systems, without permission in writing from the author. The only exception is by a reviewer, who may quote short excerpts in a review.

This book is a work of fiction. Names, characters, places, and incidents either are products of the author's imagination or are used fictitiously. Any resemblance to actual persons, living or dead, events, or locales is entirely coincidental.

Visit my website at www.danicafavorite.com

Printed in the United States of America

First Printing: June 2017

ISBN-13 978-1-945079-01-6

Chapter One

Medical equipment. Gizmos and gadgets that belonged in a hospital, not in a person's home.

Andrew Bigby pushed past the miscellaneous items stacked along the hallway by the back door. He took a deep breath as he walked further into the room. His grandmother was not that sick. In fact, when he got into the living room, there sat Gram in her favorite chair, sipping a cup of tea.

He bent and kissed her on top of her head. "What's all this stuff, Gram?"

Gram set her cup of tea on the rickety round table his great uncle such-and-such had made and looked up at him with a resigned expression on her face.

"That stupid caseworker Matilda Talcott. The nurse told her I wasn't doing what I'm supposed to be doing for therapy. So now they've got some other nurse who's going to come in and take care of me. They think I need all this junk."

A couple months before, Gram's children, a.k.a. Andrew's parents, aunts and uncles, had decided to try to take over the family farm after Gram broke her leg in a riding accident. While their initial bid was not successful, they had succeeded in getting Gram assigned a caseworker. The caseworker was supposed to make sure that Andrew, his sister Allie, and his cousin Caroline were not abusing Gram, or exercising undue influence over her to gain control over her finances.

Andrew shook his head. What a joke. Only the not funny kind. Just a ridiculous waste of everyone's time. This wasn't about concern for Gram's care, but the rest of his family being angry at not getting their fair share of Gram's farm. Though the caseworker agreed that none of them were abusing Gram, nor taking advantage of her in any way, she kept butting in when it came to Gram's medical care. Apparently the way Andrew and his family took care of Gram—as in, treating her like a grown woman capable of making her own decisions—wasn't what the caseworker wanted. Gram didn't like modern medicine, and that was just fine by Andrew. Unfortunately the caseworker didn't agree.

Gram pointed at the other side of the room, where Andrew saw a petite woman who barely looked like she could lift a feed sack, let alone do any of the stuff Gram needed, sat.

"Hi," she said. "I'm Layla Avila."

"I assume you're the new nurse. I'm Andrew Bigby."

This was the third nurse the caseworker had sent to their home to take care of Gram. Most of them got frustrated with Gram's eccentricities and quit. He wasn't going to bother getting to know this one either. After all, she'd be gone just as quickly as she'd arrived.

He'd admit she was kind of cute, though, if a man were to be interested in dating. Andrew had given up on admiring a pretty girl a long time ago. Still, there was something about that long, silky hair and dark eyes . . .

No. Focus. Andrew took a deep breath and tried to smile at her. "What's with all the equipment?"

Layla folded her arms across her chest. "I'm afraid that's privileged information. HIPAA laws and all that."

So she was one of those. Fighting the urge to roll his eyes, Andrew turned to Gram.

"Would you like to do the honors, or shall I?"

Gram grinned. They'd had this conversation a time or two, and by now, a person would think that someone would have noted it in her records.

"We speak freely in this house. All the lawyer documents have been signed. I don't keep secrets from my grandchildren. Now, my blood-sucking children, well, that's another story."

This time, Andrew didn't bother hiding the groan. "I thought we were working on being nice, Gram. Remember your blood pressure."

"I am thinking of my blood pressure," Gram said. "Keeping it all in only makes it worse. I don't know how Edward and I raised such a bunch of greedy ingrates. Except for Adam, of course, may he rest in peace."

Andrew came alongside Gram and put his hand on her shoulder, squeezing it. Gram had been mentioning her late son more often lately, and he wondered if being forced to slow down was making her more aware of her losses. Andrew liked to keep busy for the same reason—keeping the pain of his own unbearable loss at a dull ache.

He'd only met his Uncle Adam a few times before Adam was

killed in an accident. Since Andrew had only been a child, he didn't remember his uncle, except that he'd made Andrew laugh, and since Adam's death, nothing in the family had been the same.

Some people thought Gram was crazy, and maybe she was a little bit. But grief did funny things to people, and while Andrew didn't remember a lot about how Gram was before Adam's death, he knew firsthand how the death of a loved one changed a person. Poor Gram had lost a husband and a son. He'd only lost half that much, and some days, Andrew felt like the struggle to breathe was almost not worth the effort. He hadn't even gotten the chance to walk down the aisle with Mykel. She'd died too soon. If this was the grief he felt having been robbed of a life with her, how much more so did Gram feel her losses? No, he wouldn't judge her like so many did.

Instead, he gave her shoulder another squeeze. "Let's do what we can to keep you around for a while longer, all right?"

Gram smiled up at him with watery eyes. "Only the Good Lord knows how long we'll be on this earth, but I reckon I have so many questions to ask Him, that He's going to take His time calling me home. No one likes listening to an annoying old lady."

"You're not annoying, Gram." Andrew gave her another pat, then sat in one of the nearby chairs. He turned his attention to Layla. "Now that we've gotten that out of the way, why don't you explain to me what's going on? You can start with all the medical equipment in the house. Gram doesn't need all that garbage."

Layla looked at him in the same indulgent way a person looks at a child. "Your grandmother's rehab hasn't been going so well.

She's been missing her appointments. She's also starting to develop some complications from not listening to her doctors."

Andrew turned to his grandmother. "That true, Gram?"

"They want me to do yoga." The indignation on Gram's face made Andrew want to laugh. However, he knew from experience that if he did laugh, it would only make her angrier.

"Yoga, huh?"

"Do I look like a pretzel to you?"

Andrew just smiled at his grandmother. "Nope. But Gram, you've got to go to rehab. That leg of yours needs some extra care, so that it's strong enough for you to come out and help us in the garden. We're going to need your help with all those extra cucumbers you wanted planted for that new pickle recipe you're dying to try."

Gram frowned. "Mona already tried it. They're disgusting."

With a smile, Layla came towards them. "My *abuela* makes great pickles. I can ask her if she'd be willing to share the recipe."

Gram's face twisted into a scowl, and Andrew already knew what was coming. Why such a nice offer would set her off, he didn't know, but Layla would be running for the hills when it was over.

"I don't know any Abuelas. If I don't know them, then they must not be much of a cook. I know every good cook in Arcadia Valley."

Leaning in to Gram, Andrew said softly, "I believe *abuela* means grandmother in Spanish."

"Well I don't know Spanish." Gram crossed her arms and stared at Layla. "I wouldn't be able to read the recipe."

"My *abuela* is fluent in English. We use Spanish words and

endearments as a way of preserving our heritage." Layla spoke softly as she approached Gram.

"How about I bring you some of her pickles next time I come? Abuela says there isn't a food that can't be pickled, so I'll bring some regular pickles as well as one of her interesting varieties. I'm told you have rather unique food choices."

Andrew had to give Layla some credit. She was enough of an optimist to believe that she'd be coming back. He respected that. Even though he'd pretty much given up on hanging on to any optimism of his own long before this.

**

Layla was doing her best not to lose her temper with the cranky old woman in front of her. She'd been told that Enid Bigby was a nasty woman with a tongue as sharp as a razor. They'd specifically asked Layla to take the case because they knew Layla was good with difficult patients. As far as she could tell, the difficulty wasn't going to be with Enid, but with getting her grandchildren to stop coddling her. Already she could see the apologies on Andrew's lips for his grandmother's behavior.

"How do I know it's not poison? Does she put gluten in it? Does she know any of my children, who are trying to kill me?"

One of Enid's previous nurses had put in her notes that the elderly woman was paranoid about a number of strange things. Clearly she hadn't been exaggerating. Yet as Layla looked at Enid's eyes, she could see genuine fear that she thought someone was trying to hurt her.

"Why do you think your children are trying to kill you?" Layla asked pleasantly, hoping to defuse the situation.

Enid glared at her. "Because they hate me. And they hate the farm. They want to destroy everything we've worked for."

"I'm sure that's not true." She looked over at Andrew, who shook his head.

"You'd think," he said. "But no. I've heard every single one of them say they hate their mother. And they also hate the farm. I don't think they're trying to kill Gram, but they have been trying to put her in a home for years."

"Which will kill me," Enid wailed, pounding the floor with her cane.

Andrew let out a long sigh. "I told you. No one is putting you in a home. Me, Allie, and Caroline have all promised you that. We'll do whatever it takes to keep you right here where you belong."

And there it was. The one thing Layla needed to do her job. She couldn't help smiling as she crossed the last few steps to Enid.

"Then we should have no problem. As long as you do everything I say, you get to stay right here. But if you continue to be noncompliant with your treatment, I'll have no choice but to recommend to Ms. Talcott that you be admitted for inpatient care."

Her words, however, did not have the desired effect. Enid smiled as she leaned back against her chair. "You can recommend, but you can't force me. I know my rights. And I have my lawyer on speed dial."

Andrew looked at Layla sympathetically. "Just so you know, she's not bluffing. We're not joking about how aggressively our family has been working to get Gram out of the way. She knows her rights inside and out, and now that Caroline is engaged to a lawyer, there's not a lot that gets by Gram."

The grandson meant well, as most of them did. But he obviously didn't understand that by helping he was only making things worse. And yet, she couldn't help admiring how strongly he fought for the old woman. Most people didn't have that depth of loyalty.

"If the family is being as aggressive as you say, then why aren't you doing more to help your grandmother be in compliance with her medical care, so that your family has no ammunition against her?"

"Because the doctors are all in on it!" Enid jumped up from her chair and immediately lost her balance, forcing her to sit back down.

Though many nurses would rush to her assistance, Layla could tell that Enid would only resent it, and her, even more as a result.

So instead, Layla kept her attention on the grandson. Weird to think of someone near her own age as someone's grandson, but she was someone's granddaughter, so it should have made sense. Except there was something different about the man before her. He seemed older, ancient even, in the way he looked at her. But that was ridiculous, since Andrew Bigby was young, and, if she were honest, handsome. His sandy-blond hair was tousled the way a model's might be, only Layla could tell that it was from the wind, and not hundreds of dollars of product. Though he was properly clothed, she could sense that he was muscular, not from hours in a gym, but hours on the farm. The weathered hands that tended to his grandmother were evidence of the hard work he did every day.

Exactly the kind of man she could bring home to her family

and they would approve of. At least her father would. He'd done everything he could to shed his Mexican heritage, and resented the fact that Layla had wanted to reconnect with her mother's side of the family, who embraced being Mexican, rather than trying to abandon it. Connecting with her Mexican relatives had brought a missing piece back into her life.

Which was why Layla had no interest in dating at this point in time. She already had too much on her plate with figuring out her new family dynamic-learning all the new people and customs. It was still strange to her to have cousins dropping by her apartment at all hours and dragging her out to family events. Besides, she couldn't date someone so closely connected to a patient.

Could she understand Andrew's dogged desire to keep his grandmother happy? Absolutely. But keeping her happy and keeping her healthy were two different things.

Layla smiled at Andrew. Her cheeks would hurt tonight from so many forced smiles, but sometimes the job required it.

"Do you think the doctors are in on the plot to harm your grandmother?"

He sat back in his chair. "Leave me out of it."

"Interesting." She shook her head at him. "You say you care about her and would do anything to keep her out of a home, but when I ask for your honest assessment of the situation, you refuse to give an opinion?"

Enid chortled. It figured she'd enjoy someone else being called out for a change.

"Fine." Andrew leaned forward again. "You want to know what I think? I think the doctors and the nurses have spent zero time figuring out what Gram wants, and how they can be partners in her healing. Instead, they're forcing their own agendas on her without even trying to see things from her perspective. Do I think that's coming from my relatives? No. I think it's a problem with the medical community in general. You play God with people's lives without considering the impact it has on those lives. So maybe, instead of forcing her to do a bunch of stuff she doesn't want to do, like yoga, you can figure out things she can do instead that will achieve the same objective."

Suddenly, Layla didn't feel so confident in her job anymore. As much as she hated to admit it, he had a point. She'd come in with her plan, and was prepared to implement it, knowing that Enid Bigby was a stubborn old woman who argued with everyone over everything. But was that the whole picture?

"All right then," Layla said, looking over at Enid. "We all know that you've got some health issues to deal with. But you're not taking your medicine, not doing your physical therapy, and making life difficult for everyone who tries to help you. So tell me how you think you're going to heal when you're literally doing none of the things necessary for your healing."

Then she looked over at Andrew and gave him a small smile. Maybe he was right that people weren't looking at what his grandmother wanted. But since they all had the same goal of getting her well again, perhaps now he would see that she wasn't the enemy here.

Why she cared so much about what Andrew Bigby thought . . . Layla shook her head. It was just because he had so much power in Enid's life. But even as she offered that excuse, a tiny voice inside her called her a liar.

Chapter Two

She had guts, Andrew would give her that. People generally didn't give it back to Gram the way Layla had just done. Maybe someone like Layla was exactly what Gram needed, instead of all the medical personnel she scared off.

He half-listened as Gram rattled off all the herbal things she was doing to deal with her health problems. Andrew tried not to yawn. He'd been up late the previous night with Caroline and her fiancé, Hayden going over the finances for the expansion of Bigby Farm. Hayden's plan was to use Andrew's tiny house as a model for creating a village of tiny houses for people to come and experience a real working farm for themselves.

But honestly, Andrew didn't know where any of them were going to find the time or the energy to deal with farm guests. They were already in over their heads with campers for the day camp at Bigby Farm. In years past, Gram had helped out, but with her broken leg she was crankier than usual, and Caroline was afraid that she'd scare the children. Allie had picked up more shifts at the Gas N' Shop, which made no sense, except that Allie felt like she owed it to Dan, the owner, to help out when he was short-staffed. But maybe if Allie didn't pick up those shifts then Dan would be more motivated to hire someone else. Which was none of Andrew's business, except that it meant that he was helping out more with the kids instead of puttering around the farm, taking care of things that didn't involve dealing with the public.

This time, he couldn't help the yawn that escaped.

Caroline was supposed to be interviewing a few more helpers this week. Hopefully, she'd like them, and they'd pass their background checks so that Andrew could get back to his regular work. The tractor was acting up again, but between watching the kids, setting up the activities for the camp, cleaning up afterward, and making sure Gram didn't use her shotgun to send this latest nurse packing, he hadn't had a chance to take the engine apart.

Andrew yawned again.

It wasn't that the kids were so bad, actually. He liked kids. Just not for eight hours a day, five days a week, with tours to run on Saturday. Which was silly, because had Mykel lived, they'd probably have at least half a dozen by now, and people didn't get a break from their own kids.

Except when they sent them to the day camp.

He should be grateful for this chance to interact with children, since he wasn't going to have any now. When Mykel died, so had his desire for a family of his own. His desire for a lot of things had died, and mostly, he just wanted to be left alone to tinker on things on the farm.

Andrew closed his eyes. He really should be paying attention, because this was important, but . . .

"Andrew!"

He woke with a start at Gram's voice.

"I can't hear her over your snoring."

He glanced at Layla, who wore an amused expression. So much for trying to be discreet.

"Sorry, I was up too late with Caroline and Hayden."

Gram shook her head. "Where are those two, anyway?"

"Meeting with the pastor to go over wedding details."

"Why wasn't I invited? I should be there to help plan things."

Hayden took a deep breath before answering her. They'd had this conversation several times, but Gram either honestly didn't remember—in which case, he didn't want to know, because it would only give people like Layla more ammunition against her— or, this was just Gram being difficult again because she didn't like the answer she was given.

"Caroline wants to plan the whole thing herself. She wants you to focus on getting well, so you can dance at her reception."

Then Andrew turned his attention back to Layla. "You want motivation for her? How about Caroline's wedding? Get Gram out of her cast and off the cane, so she can dance and thumb her nose at all the people who said she wasn't going to walk properly again."

Layla gave him a long, hard look. "She's got to be willing to do the work."

"That she does," Andrew said, looking at Gram. "It's your choice. So do it or not do it, but you'll be suffering the consequences when you're in a wheelchair at the wedding and everyone is smothering you, trying to help."

Gram made a face, and Andrew knew his words had done the trick. That was the worst part about the situation right now.

Gram hated all the attention over her injury. Yet she didn't seem to want to do any of the things that would get rid of all the attention.

Then Gram held up a bottle of pills. "I suppose you're going to tell me I have to take these, too."

"What are they?"

"You're aware that your grandmother has diabetes and refuses insulin, correct? These won't completely make things better, but the doctor believes they should help."

He stared at Layla. "He believes?"

"Yes. This particular drug has a very high success rate."

"What about diet and exercise?"

Layla shrugged. "From what I can tell, your grandmother's diet is fine for diabetics. No sugar, no processed foods. She can't exercise until she gets that cast off, so this is the next best thing."

Every warning bell in Andrew's head went off. So many of Layla's words sounded exactly like what he'd heard from Mykel's doctors. And where had that gotten her?

The worst part was, they'd blindly trusted those doctors. After all, they were doctors. They knew, right? Wrong. Had Andrew only dug a little deeper, done some research, they might have found that there were better options for treating Mykel's cancer. Maybe Gram didn't have cancer, but diabetes was serious. Too serious to be messing around with drugs they thought might help without having all the information.

"I'll need to do some research first. What about the supplements Gram is taking? Can't those help diabetes?"

Layla gave him a look to rival one of Gram's best glares. "And what are you, a doctor?"

"No. But I can use the internet just as well as one."

"And your degree is in what?"

Her condescending tone grated on his nerves. It wasn't as though she was a doctor, either.

"I have an MBA."

Layla continued to glare. "And that qualifies you to do what with medicine, a doctor's taxes? Maybe the billing, or the books?"

She thought she was so smart. Ha! Maybe he hadn't gone to medical school, but when Mykel got sick, he'd spent plenty of time learning about medicine. His education came from the School of Hard Knocks.

He returned Layla's condescending look. "You're not a doctor, either."

"But I do have a bachelor's in nursing."

Her words were sharp, like he'd touched a nerve. Good. Because all of his were on fire.

"So then why are you doing home health care, which pays a fraction of what you'd get at the hospital? I know for a fact that none of Gram's previous nurses had such credentials. I researched them all."

Her eyes widened at his words. Even better. Let her know she was on watch.

Layla squared her shoulders. "My career choices are none of your business. I'm here to do a job, which is to take care of your grandmother. I can't do that with you arguing with me. You don't want her to take medicine for her diabetes? Fine. While you're playing doctor online, why don't you also look up the complications your grandmother can have as a result of letting her diabetes remain untreated? Then you get back to me on what you prefer."

Layla stood up and walked over to the counter where Gram kept her vitamins and supplements. "Also, while you're at it, look up these. Because two of them are known to increase the negative side-effects of diabetes, and another two are not supposed to be taken together. I don't know who your grandmother is getting her nutritional advice from, but it may well be what ends up killing her."

She might believe in what she was saying, but Layla had no idea what she was talking about.

It wasn't the cancer that had killed Mykel, but the combination of drugs they'd given her. The doctors had said there were risks, of course. But they'd missed the part about how those risks were higher for Mykel.

That was the trouble with all these medical people. They thought their pills were the miracle cure, and they totally ignored anything else.

"Stop!" Gram stood, balancing on her cane. "Those aren't all my vitamins. Some are Caroline's, some are Allie's, and I think Hayden has some. All of my vitamins and supplements are listed in my chart, and I've been honest about what I take. I don't like pills of any sort, and I can use the computer just as well as any of you. My friend Mona taught me how to look things up on the CDC website, so I can weigh the risks and benefits for myself."

Gram looked over at him, and her eyes were filled with sympathy. She knew what he'd gone through when Mykel got sick. And she'd watched her husband lose his own battle with cancer.

"You leave this to me, you hear, Andrew? No looking things up and worrying yourself, all right?"

He nodded, suddenly overcome with the weight of having to deal with another loved one's medical care. Gram might not be dying, but she did have a serious medical condition, and it was enough to make him worry. Even if she did tell him not to.

"Now you go out to the barn and get to work on that tractor. It won't fix itself."

Though Andrew hated to leave Gram alone, he recognized the space she was offering him. Everything about this conversation with Layla had brought up pieces of grief he hadn't been prepared for. If he stayed in this room much longer, he might suffocate from the heaviness surrounding him.

Mumbling his goodbyes as best as he could without breaking down, Andrew fled to the barn and the safety of a machine that would never fully die, because it could always be fixed. Unlike the people he loved.

**

Layla watched Andrew leave. She'd been out of line in how she'd spoken to him, but she hadn't been able to help herself. He'd pushed all her buttons, especially the ones she'd thought safe from people messing with.

"Don't mind him," Enid said quietly. "He means well. Andrew is generally the kindest, most loving human being you'll ever meet. A great feat, given his upbringing. But he's protective of those he loves, and this is a very touchy area for him."

Nothing would have surprised Layla more than the old woman's words. Gone was the nasty exterior, and all Layla could see was the deep love of a grandmother for her grandson.

"You need the medicine," Layla said.

Enid nodded slowly. "I just don't understand why I have diabetes. I eat right, and until my accident, I got plenty of exercise. How could this happen to me?"

More insight into Enid and her resistance to all the treatment. It was easy to be in denial when you didn't fully understand the facts.

"Some people are just more naturally predisposed to diabetes. Even with proper diet and exercise, some people still manage to have it. You haven't done anything wrong. It's just that, sometimes, your body has other ideas. Were it not for your healthy diet and exercise, you might have shown signs earlier."

Layla smiled at the older woman and sat in the chair Andrew had vacated. "Did your doctor give you any pamphlets or information about diabetes?"

"I threw them in the trash," Enid said. "I didn't believe I could have that stupid disease."

"That's not going to get you any better. I've got some information in my bag for you to read at your leisure, but for now, let's discuss where we go from here."

As Layla explained her treatment to the older woman, she realized that some of Enid's nasty and irrational behavior could easily be attributed to her untreated diabetes. Perhaps she, along with so many others, had misjudged the woman.

Layla stole a glance at the door Andrew had exited. It would be easy to dismiss him as being one more ignorant man who relied on the internet more than his doctor's advice.

But his words had been tinged with a deep sadness, and when

he'd left the room, she could have sworn he was on the verge of a breakdown. All too often, people looked at the surface of things without looking into the deeper causes.

Andrew had been right to call her out for not trying to find a more cooperative solution for Enid. However, he'd wounded her pride, especially when he'd correctly pointed out that someone with her degree and training didn't generally work for a basic home healthcare company. But that was her own private pain. One she didn't like to even think about.

Though it was a good reminder of why, even though there was something about Andrew that drew her, she didn't get involved with patients or their families.

Layla checked Enid's vitals, noting that while her blood pressure was elevated, it wasn't dangerously so. The doctor had put in the file that this seemed to be the case with Enid, so part of the difficulty in her care was managing her stress, knowing that medical things stressed her out.

"Tell me about yourself," Layla said, making some notes on Enid's file. "Your grandson accused me of pursuing my agenda, so tell me about what you want. What matters to you? Your granddaughter's wedding?"

Once again, she found herself looking at where Andrew had been. They'd really sparked off one another, but in a way that surprised her. She'd clashed with patients' families before, but none had ever called her out in a way that made her think deeper about patient care. Clearly, her words had affected him as well.

Enid seemed to sense where Layla's thoughts had taken her. "He's a good boy. I know he thought reminding me about Caroline's wedding would get me excited, but I don't care about a stupid wedding. That's why they didn't invite me to go with them to the pastor's. She told me she wanted a small wedding with no fuss. But now that she and Camille, her mother, have made up, suddenly this wedding is turning into one of those fancy to-dos that I despise."

Enid crossed her arms over her chest and slumped in her chair. "Camille probably got to go."

Layla knelt in front of her. "Is Camille one of the children trying to put you in a home?"

The older woman nodded, her eyes filling with tears again. No one had noted any signs of depression in Enid's charts, but they might have been overlooking it because they were so focused on her sour attitude.

"So Camille and Caroline made up, but not you and Camille? That has to be hard, being at odds with your daughter, knowing she's repaired her relationship with her daughter."

"All of my children hate me. They resent growing up poor, and think I'm being selfish for not selling the farm to a developer who will make them rich. But they're all doing just fine. Camille's husband, Stephen, has so much money he could use it as toilet paper. It's all about the dollars and cents, not about caring for one another. Their hatred of me has been the only thing keeping them together all these years."

Tears ran down Enid's face, and Layla realized that much of her hostility probably came from feeling abandoned by her family. Of course, if Enid was nasty to her children, they probably didn't want to come around. Which turned into a vicious cycle of Enid lashing out because of her feelings, and them not wanting to visit because of Enid's attitude.

Layla took her hand and squeezed it. "Maybe, if we showed your family that you were taking care of yourself, and you were feeling better, you could reconcile."

"Reconcile?" Enid pulled her hand away. "Why should it be up to me, when they're the ones in the wrong? They all owe me a big apology."

So much for trying to appeal to her tender side. Except that, written across Enid's face were lines that spoke of deep wounds. Layla knew nothing of the situation. And it wasn't her job to get involved. She was just trying to find a way to convince Enid to go along with her care plan.

However, Enid's mood swings and possible depression made Layla wonder if she had seen a counselor. Perhaps counseling, combined with the right medication, would help Enid's frame of mind so that she'd be more willing to participate in her recovery.

Layla glanced at Enid's chart. No mention of any mental health referrals.

"Have you thought about seeing a therapist," Layla asked casually. "I have a friend who's great at helping sort through family issues."

Enid reached for her cane. "You're just like everyone else! Trying to be nice to me, then using that to get information to suggest I'm crazy. I'm not crazy! Only crazy people go to therapy!"

Clearly she'd pushed too hard, too soon. Layla took a deep breath as she stepped back. "I didn't say that you're crazy. I just said that a therapist might help you figure out your family problems, so you feel more at peace. I've used her for my own family issues, which is why I thought she might be able to help you. She definitely helped me."

Using her cane as support, Enid stood, her face mottled with rage. "You might be crazy, but I'm not. The problem with my family isn't me, it's them. They're the ones who need therapy. Not appreciating everything I've done for them. Trying to take away my farm."

The back door opened, and Andrew entered, slightly out of breath. "What's going on in here? I heard shouting."

He didn't wait for an answer as he ran to his grandmother and put his arms around her. "Gram, are you all right?"

Enid looked up at him, the teary-eyed expression back on her face. "She said I'm crazy."

Before Layla could formulate the words to explain what had happened, Andrew turned his gaze on her.

"Get out. I should have never left her alone with you. She's an old woman, can't you have a little sensitivity?"

"But I didn't-" Layla started to defend herself, but Andrew shook his head.

"Just go. I'll be in touch with your supervisor."

Even though Layla had done nothing wrong, his words chilled her. Any report would have to be investigated, and sometimes, just having an investigation on her record could cause trouble. All she'd wanted to do was create a good life for herself, connecting with her family. But one cantankerous case could mess it all up.

So much for her new start in Arcadia Valley.

Chapter Three

Layla dipped the teabag into her teacup a few times as she stared at the phone. She really should call her supervisor to let him know what had happened. Jack probably already had gotten an earful from the Bigbys. She shook her head. No. He'd have called after getting off the phone from them.

Ugh. She was sitting on a ticking time bomb, and it would probably go off anytime soon. Better to try to defuse it now, rather than let it get all over everything.

A knock sounded at the door, and Layla went to open it. She didn't know many people in Arcadia Valley since moving here, other than her *abuela* and the various cousins and relatives whose faces were all a blur and still didn't match any of the names she knew. But sometimes, the little girl in the building would stop by and invite her to come work in the community garden. Maybe that would get her mind off things.

Layla opened the door. Andrew stood there, holding a bouquet of flowers. She recognized them as being from Blossoms by Akers. She'd just been walking down that way earlier in the day when she'd seen a similar bouquet in the window. At the time she'd admired it, wishing she had flowers like that to brighten up her tiny little apartment. Whoever had arranged it had used a variety of flowers she wasn't familiar with, and she'd liked the way they were unique but colorful. And here it was, just a couple hours later, and Andrew was here with them.

The question was, why?

"What are you doing here?"

He held out the bouquet. "I was rude to you earlier today. I shouldn't have been so harsh with you. My comments were less about you than they were about me and my fears. I shouldn't have let them take control of me. And, I should have at least heard you out before accusing you. I'm not calling your supervisor. Gram told me the full story, and clearly she and I both overreacted. I'm sorry."

Layla had never heard such a sincere apology before. The expression on Andrew's face told her that his words and actions came from a great deal of soul-searching. A great deal of wrestling over what to say and what to do. Words like that were not the kind of thing a person easily dismissed.

Even though they had butted heads earlier, there was something about Andrew Bigby that Layla liked. Okay, fine. So he was pretty cute. But it was more than that. He'd looked at his grandmother with such tenderness and concern that it was hard not to like the man. Plus, the way he actively involved himself with her care showed that he had a deeply loving heart.

Knowing so few people in Arcadia Valley, it seemed like Andrew Bigby would be a good person to start with making friends.

"Would you like to come in for a cup of tea? I just made some, and the water's still hot."

Andrew shook his head. "I'd like to, if only to smooth the waters between us. But to be honest, I don't think it's a good idea."

What was that about? It seemed like their every interaction made Layla want to ask more questions of him. To get to know him better. To understand. But she'd gone as far as politeness dictated. To do more would be crossing a line she couldn't cross. She'd spent too much of her life chasing people who didn't want her.

Smiling at him, she said, "It's okay. I understand. Thank you for the flowers. It means a lot. I accept your apology."

Andrew nodded slowly, opened his mouth like he was going to say something, then closed it. Stillness hung between them for a moment, then Andrew finally said, "I appreciate that. I'll try not to let my issues get in the way of your care for my grandmother."

"It's really touching how much you love her. I wish more people were so devoted to their grandparents' health needs."

Andrew shrugged. "Honestly, I don't understand why everyone isn't. Sure, Gram has her rough edges, but don't we all? Loving someone is about loving the good and the bad. We all have both, so if you could only love the good in someone, none of us would be able to love anyone."

Once again Layla was struck by the depth of Andrew's character. He was the kind of man she'd always thought she'd like to have in her life. She'd spent a long time thinking such a man didn't exist. Yet here he was, and he was completely off-limits.

"I hadn't thought about it that way," she said, taking in his face in more detail for the first time.

She'd been right in pegging him as young but ancient. The lines on his face spoke of a life that hadn't been easy. She supposed that must be true if he supported his grandmother while his parents were trying to put her in a home.

Family estrangement was difficult on anyone, and obviously the Bigby family had been forced to take sides.

"Gram says she defended me to you, and I appreciate that. I'm not perfect, obviously, but I try to be a decent human being. I'm sorry that I showed you my ugly side. You should know that she's not all bad, either. Actually, she's pretty wonderful once you get to know her."

Layla couldn't help herself. She gestured once again to the interior of her apartment. "Are you sure I can't tempt you with a cup of tea? I'd really love to hear more about your family. See how I can help your grandmother. I honestly don't think she's crazy. But sounds like you're all in a tough situation, and working through some of that will do a lot for her health."

Andrew shook his head. "I appreciate the offer, but I can't. It's not you, it's me. I don't spend time alone with women who aren't family."

She stared at him. One more puzzle she didn't understand about this man.

He seemed to sense her confusion, because he continued. "Our pastor gave a sermon once that had a profound impact on me and how I treat women. I don't establish personal relationships with them because it might give them ideas that I'm interested in them romantically. It's taking his advice a little far, but I don't ever want to be in a position to make a woman feel like I've been leading her on. I'm not your friend, and I'm not a potential boyfriend. I have no intention of ever getting married, and it would be wrong for me to date or otherwise indicate someone might have a chance at my heart."

Wow. Layla wasn't sure even how to process his words. It was admirable how he knew his mind, but it seemed like he closed himself off from a lot of wonderful possibilities.

"It's just a cup of tea. I'm not expecting a marriage proposal," she said, trying to sound encouraging. "Surely we're adult enough to talk about your grandmother's care without falling in love."

Andrew chuckled softly. "I'm not much of a catch, that's for sure. I mean, I live in a tiny house on my grandmother's farm, and I make just enough to have the basics. And that's all I want. All I need, really. A woman wants more than I have to give."

The more Layla talked to Andrew, the more she found herself liking him. Not, as she said, to want a marriage proposal, but enough that she could see him as being the kind of friend she'd been wanting in her life. His blunt speech, while it might be a turn-off to some, made her feel like she could trust him. She was tired of being told what people thought she wanted to hear instead of the truth.

"I would think a woman would mostly just want love. Surely you have that to give."

Layla smiled at him, hoping to show that he didn't need to be afraid of her, or any woman for that matter. He'd obviously been burned pretty badly, poor guy.

Andrew scowled. "That's where you're wrong. I have nothing,

literally nothing, in my heart to give anyone. Gram, Allie, Caroline, that's it. I suppose I should extend that to Hayden, but honestly, that's about as wide as my circle is going to get. Allie might marry someday, I guess. Though I can't see a man being worthy of her. But that's probably the big brother in me talking."

Had Layla been on a date, she definitely would have read the hands-off signal. Some women might take it as a challenge, but she wasn't interested in having to work so hard to get a man's attention. Hadn't she already learned her lesson? Not that she wanted Andrew's attention, of course. She was interested in him for purely professional reasons-helping his grandmother.

Except, as she saw the sorrow in his eyes, she had to wonder if Enid wasn't the only Bigby in need of a little TLC.

**

Andrew walked into his favorite Mexican restaurant, El Corazon. After his meeting with Layla, he needed something to stop his whirling mind. There wasn't anything guac and chips couldn't fix. Well, he supposed that wasn't entirely true, but he'd spent a good many months after Mykel's death consuming the substance. It certainly hadn't hurt.

"Hey Andrew," his friend Javier, whose family owned the restaurant, said as Andrew walked in the door. "How's everything at the farm?"

He grinned. Maybe it wasn't so much the guac, but the company. Javier always had a way of lifting a person's spirits without even knowing. Andrew had been too busy with Gram and the farm lately for the men's group at church, so it was nice to see an old friend.

He noticed Pastor Harris sitting at one of the tables as if to further confirm the idea that he'd been missing way too much church lately. Well, that wasn't true. He had been going to church. Every Sunday as always. But it seemed like one of the children's classes was always short a teacher and someone would ask him if he wouldn't mind substituting. Of course Andrew said yes. He always promised himself he'd listen to the sermon online later, yet he never seemed to find the time.

That seemed to be the theme of his life lately. Not finding the time.

"Hey Pastor." He walked over to the table where the pastor was sitting alone, eating a bowl of guac and chips. Apparently Andrew wasn't the only one who thought guac could cure any problem.

"Andrew. Nice to see you." The pastor started to stand, but Andrew waved him off.

"Don't get up on account of me. You should enjoy your food. I just thought I would say hi, since it seems like I've been so busy lately I haven't gotten to say hi to anyone."

Pastor Harris grinned. "Yes. I hear the day camp is busier than ever."

Andrew nodded. "There just aren't a lot of childcare options for children on break. Caroline is such a softy that she never seems to be able to say no when we're at capacity. So she says yes, sends a little prayer that she'll find someone else to help her, and it always seems to work out."

The pastor chuckled. "That sounds like Caroline."

Javier walked over to him. "Want a table, or are you the person Pastor Harris is supposed to be meeting?"

29

Andrew shook his head. "A table for me is fine, thank you." Then he turned to the pastor and gave him apologetic look. "I'm sorry, I don't want to interrupt."

Pastor Harris smiled at him. "You're not interrupting at all. The person I'm meeting hasn't arrived yet. I got a text saying he was running a little late. But I was hungry, so I decided to indulge."

The door opened, and a harried young man entered the restaurant. He looked around frantically, then his eyes zeroed in on the pastor, and he darted over to the table.

"It was nice seeing you, Pastor. I'll leave you to your appointment." Andrew gave him a smile, then turned to Javier. "Now if you could get me set up at a table of my own with some of that guac and chips, I would be most appreciative."

"No problem." Javier clapped him on the back. "Molly thinks everyone wants some new innovation, but I'm like you. I appreciate an old standby. Something to drink?"

"I'll stick with water. I'm a simple guy, and water always suits me just fine. Plain water."

Andrew chuckled to himself as he thought about how symbolic his choice of plain water was especially after his conversation with Layla. He told her he was a simple man, and his choice of water seem to prove it. Simple, uncomplicated, basic. Nothing a woman would be interested in. And he wasn't interested in women.

"I didn't think water was so funny," Javier said.

"Sorry. Private joke."

Javier led him to a table. "Have a seat." He waved at one of the servers and repeated Andrew's order to her. Then he took the seat opposite Andrew.

"Now you can tell me that joke. It's been a while since I've seen you."

Andrew grinned and shook his head. "It's nothing. I met this woman today, and she was so infuriating, but in an oddly refreshing way."

"You met a woman? That isn't nothing."

"Nothing like that. She's Gram's new home healthcare nurse. Unlike all the others, she pushes a lot of buttons. Mine and Gram's. She means well, and her heart seems to be in the right place, but there's so much she doesn't understand."

"And that has you in here, seeking comfort in our guacamole."

"It's a habit I guess. Plus you have to admit that you have the best guac in the universe."

"It is pretty good. But I find it interesting that this woman has had such an effect on you."

"Don't you start. I had to explain to her my policy on becoming friends with women. I don't want to have to remind you of it too. That door is closed. Barred. Chained. And for good measure, it has a steel door bolted over it."

"If you say so. But you're arguing this one a little too hard. She must've really gotten to you."

She had, that was the thing. Andrew couldn't explain it to himself, so how could he explain it to his friend?

"Or maybe I'm just exhausted. Those kids are driving me nuts."

"At least you get to send them home every night," Javier said, chuckling.

He started to say something else, but as the door opened, he stood, completely ignoring Andrew.

"Layla. I'm so glad you're finally here."

Before Andrew knew what was happening, Javier had pulled out one of the chairs at their table and gestured towards it. "Please sit. Come meet my good friend Andrew. We've got guacamole and chips on the way. I'm glad you've finally stopped in."

Andrew tried not to stare at the woman he'd just run out on. True, he'd exited with a modicum of grace, but mostly he felt sick at how she'd been trying to be so nice to him, and he'd acted like a scared teenager with his first crush. Which was crazy, because he didn't have a crush on Layla. Couldn't have. His heart firmly belonged to Mykel, which is where it would remain, now that she was gone.

Still, how was he supposed to pretend that everything was all right with him when something in him had shifted?

It would be rude for Andrew to leave. Even more rude to dismiss someone that Javier was clearly so happy to see. And yet, all he wanted to do was eat his guac in peace.

Layla didn't act like anything was wrong as she took the seat Javier offered her. She smiled warmly at Javier, then Andrew.

"We've already met. I'm his grandmother's nurse."

"Is that right?" Javier said, looking at Andrew knowingly.

Great. His friend didn't know anything, but now he thought he did. And the merciless teasing would never end.

"Yes," Layla said, her brown eyes sparkling.

Sparkling? Andrew wasn't supposed to notice things like that. Maybe he was affected by hunger. Yes, that was it. He was faint from hunger.

He looked over at Javier. "How long is that guac going to take anyway? I'm starving."

One of the waitress brought over a bowl of chips and a bowl of salsa. "This will get you started," she said.

Andrew took a chip and dipped it, then promptly stuffed his face so he wouldn't be able obligated to participate in any conversation. Fortunately, Javier didn't press the matter.

"Layla is one of our cousins. She recently moved to Arcadia Valley to get to know us all, isn't that something?"

"How many cousins do you have anyway? It seems like I can't go anywhere without running into one of them."

Javier shrugged. "We have a large family. And extended family. It's good to have so many people who care about you."

At least Javier didn't remind Andrew of his own large clan. The two families were so different, but everyone liked to make the comparison. Where Javier's family was warm and loving, Andrew's was more like a scene from *The Hunger Games*. The only relations he trusted were Gram, Caroline, and Allie.

Andrew shrugged. "Maybe for you, but I have my limits. With Caroline getting married and my aunt and uncle spending more time on the farm, I pretty much have my fill of relatives."

Javier laughed. "But that's where you're wrong. Family is a treasured gift, and just because yours isn't getting along right now doesn't mean someday you won't need them. We haven't seen Layla since she was five or six years old. Now she's here, and it's good that we can be here to support her in a new town."

Then Javier looked over Layla and smiled. "I know it's overwhelming for you, going from having no relatives, no connections, to having all of us surround you. But I hope you know we mean well. And I haven't seen Abuela so happy in a long time. When your parents took you away from here, we were all very sad."

Andrew watched the expression flutter across Layla's face. Just as quickly as the urge came to try to analyze it, he reminded himself that her situation, her past, and her family situation were none of his business. And yet, for a brief second, he wished he was capable of opening his heart to another person. There was something about Layla that he liked, something that drew him. But it didn't matter. To even entertain the idea seemed just shy of ridiculous.

Chapter Four

A week later, Layla felt like they'd finally found a comfortable routine. She'd arrive to work with Enid, Andrew would mumble some kind of awkward apology, then disappear. She'd thought their last run-in, at El Corazon, had been initially awkward, but then she'd thought they'd at least become cordial at the end.

But this avoidance routine?

Layla sighed as she pulled up to the house. What tactic would Andrew use today?

She shook her head. It didn't matter. She was here to connect with her family, not chase after a man who clearly didn't want anything to do with her. Still, as she got out of her car, she couldn't help looking around for him.

As usual, Andrew hovered near the door, pretending to fix something on it. If the door was that broken, why had she been using it every day?

But why couldn't he just say that he wanted to see her? Or try talking to her like a normal human being?

"Hello Andrew," she said, smiling.

It had become a game, her greeting him in a friendly manner, and him acting embarrassed and running away.

Why she played the game she didn't know. Except that she had some kind of pathological need to chase after men who wanted nothing to do with her. Hadn't she learned her lesson with her father? With Troy?

"Layla." He pulled the hat off his head and wiped his brow.

It was one of those Panama-type hats, which seemed out of place on an Idaho farm. Yet it suited him.

"I'm surprised you're not helping Caroline with the children. Enid tells me that today is craft day."

Andrew replaced his hat on his head. "She finally hired a couple of people. We had to pay more than I would have liked, but good help is hard to find. It's crazy. People need affordable care for their children, but you have to pay a living wage to the workers, except to do that, you have to charge more money than people can afford. Which goes against what Gram set out to do with the day camp in the first place."

He stopped suddenly, like he realized that he'd finally said more than two words to her and regretted it.

Then he shook his head. "Sorry. Not your problem. I love Gram, and I love her mission. I'm just the guy who has to help her pay for it. And some days, that really stinks."

The forlorn look on his face made Layla's heart ache, and she wanted to reach out to him. Why couldn't she be drawn to a normal man, one who didn't give weird speeches about not being alone with women so they didn't get the wrong idea?

"Why do it, then? If your grandmother's blood pressure gets any higher, we'll have no choice but to put her on medication, and I've barely convinced her to take it for her diabetes. If the camp is causing her stress as well, then perhaps you should rethink your choices."

He looked at her with the same expression he usually wore when he thought she'd just said something completely idiotic. Then he shook his head.

"I keep forgetting you're not from around here. Bigby Farm started back in 1910. Everything here goes back to the traditions that began then. Folks didn't have a lot, especially during the Depression, and both Gram's family and Gramps's family have always found ways to contribute to the community, even when they didn't have much themselves. The day camp not only helps families who need child care for their children, but it teaches kids about the rich heritage of Arcadia Valley."

Layla could appreciate the passion in Andrew's voice, especially as his eyes lit up talking about their mission. But the lines on his forehead told another story.

"But if it's causing you so much stress, and bringing friction to your family-"

"And what about the stress and friction it creates for families who have to work to keep food on the table, but don't have a safe place to bring their children while they do it?" Andrew bent and picked up the tool bag at his feet.

Looking back at her, he continued, "I appreciate what you're trying to do, and what you're saying. But this isn't just about what we want or what's best for us. Take my sister, Allie, for example. She works at the Gas N' Shop because they need help. And, as much as I hate to admit it, the money, while it's not great, gives us the capital we need to buy the supplies for her lavender business. We're hoping eventually it will make enough money to sustain itself, but right now, it's what our parents like to call, "her cute little hobby.""

Even though circumstances were slightly different, Layla could relate to having her passion demeaned. After all, wasn't that what her father had done to her with her desire to connect with her Mexican heritage? Maybe Andrew hadn't been directly affected by his parents' words, but by the lines on his face, Layla could tell that he'd taken on his sister's burden as his own.

Andrew let out a long sigh. "But they don't get it. No one does. Allie's doing wonderful things with her lavender products and essential oils. Caroline and Hayden have a well-thought-out plan for turning this farm into a learning destination. Together, we're building something great, but it takes time and patience. Which means a little stress now. In the end, though, it'll all be worth it."

He sounded so exhausted as he spoke. And everything was about his cousin and his sister. Not Layla's patient. Or him. It seemed odd to meet someone so self-sacrificing, because it was counter to what the rest of the world tended to believe in.

One more reason she liked him, and it also made her even more curious. Who was he in terms of what he wanted for himself?

"And what about you and your dreams?" she asked quietly. "What about what your grandmother wants?"

Another long sigh escaped Andrew. "This is my dream. What Gram wants. She wants to keep the family farm intact, not divided up into a subdivision or golf course or some other monstrosity that fails to honor over a hundred years of Bigby sweat and blood."

Except it didn't sound like Andrew's dream. Not with the exhaustion written all over his face.

"But what do you want? All this work surely isn't necessary to achieve those ends."

Was that despair on his face? Or something else? He looked like a man trapped, like he was used to giving those answers, but wasn't sure he believed them.

"Do you know how close we are to losing the farm every year?" He shook his head like he was disgusted. "The taxes are insane, and Gram had to take out a mortgage on the place to cover our grandfather's medical care when he got sick. We've all contributed the best we can, and I've thought about getting a job to cover the difference. But Allie's already working a job she doesn't want, Caroline's running the day camp, and that leaves me to farm it. If we're not actively farming, then the property taxes just go higher. Trust me. We've looked at all the options."

But that didn't answer what he wanted. And while it was none of her business, and she shouldn't care, Layla couldn't help herself.

"And in a perfect world, what would your dream for the farm be?"

Andrew shrugged. "Honestly? I just want to work the land, live in my tiny house, and not worry about any of this. But someone's got to. If you give Allie ten dollars, she'll spend twenty, investing in some new idea. Caroline tries, but with her heart of gold, she'd give the farm away. You have no idea the number of "scholarship" kids she accepts into the camp every session."

Then he gave a quick shake of his head. "Please don't think

poorly of them because I just said that. Those are the things I love about them. Allie's the innovator, Caroline's the giver, and I'm the guy who makes it all work out. It's how we've always been. I like the part I play. So don't think you need to come in here and fix us. Your only job is to get Gram healthy enough to run around again, bossing everyone the way she loves."

Layla thought about his words and how deeply he seemed to care for his family. About their team. She'd seen a similar dynamic with her cousins and their restaurant, but also in the other projects they pursued. What was that like, investing in a dream as a cohesive unit?

It was her turn to shake her head. This might be the Bigby family dream, but the stress of it was taking its toll-on all of them—whether they knew it or not.

"And how's your blood pressure?" Layla asked, examining the lines on his face in a new way.

"You're not my nurse. Get in there and ask Gram, since that's what you're here to do."

He had a point. And he was right. But how many times had she heard Enid express her concern over how hard her grandchildren were working?

"She worries about you. Maybe if you took better care of yourself, she'd worry less, and her blood pressure would go down. Just as things on a farm are interconnected, so, too, are members of a family. I'm going to be teaching Enid some meditation techniques today. Maybe you should join us."

Layla didn't know where that offer had come from, especially since she'd been very firmly telling herself that the last thing she needed was to get involved with Andrew Bigby. But as much as she kept telling herself to stay away, to leave him alone, she found she couldn't. Her father used to tease her for bringing home every stray and wounded animal she found, and in a way, Andrew reminded her of those animals. True, he had a family who loved him, but he still seemed . . . lost.

**

Andrew tried not to laugh at Layla's offer. But he couldn't help himself.

"Meditation? Like some weird mumbo jumbo from other religions? You know we're Christians, right? I mean, your family is too. Javier is one of the best Christians I know."

Fortunately, she didn't look offended that he'd laughed at her idea. Instead, she laughed too. Which was kind of a pretty, musical sound.

"Christians can meditate. In Philippians 4:8, it talks about the things you should think about. That's meditation. Just because the word is associated with other things doesn't mean it isn't ours. I believe in taking all things captive unto Christ and using it to the glory of His name."

Even if he wanted to come up with a retort, Andrew wasn't sure he would have been able to. How long had it been since he'd looked at the world through the lens she spoke of? Most days, he was so tired, he felt like he barely had time to think of God at all.

"I hadn't thought of it that way. I guess I can join you," he said, gesturing at the door. "Gram is probably wondering where you are."

Without waiting for her to answer, Andrew opened the door and held it for her. As soon as he stepped inside, he could hear Gram.

"It's about time! You're late, and I've been wanting to show you something."

He grinned as he watched Gram pull herself out of her chair. She wasn't a patient person on a good day, but her injury had made her even less so. She hobbled over to a nearby table, and Andrew was pleased to note that she was relying less on her cane. He hadn't seen this much progress from all of the other home health nurses combined.

"I have here Camille's old yearbook. And you know who's in it? Your mother. I didn't think Camille had any friends, but your mother wrote something nice in it to her, and I thought you might like to see it."

Andrew was glad Aunt Camille wasn't in the room to hear Gram's words. She'd been staying with them to help Caroline plan the wedding, but hopefully she was off on some other part of the farm. Even though he knew his grandmother meant them as a compliment, Aunt Camille would probably take them as an insult, and that would start . . .

"What are you going on about me now, Mother? Why can't you just give it a rest?"

He shouldn't have even thought it. Camille burst into the room from the sewing room, her eyes full of tears.

"She was saying that she realized you and Layla's mother were friends. She was trying to do something nice for Layla," Andrew said quickly, hating that once again he'd been put in the position of being a mediator.

Layla wanted so badly to dig into their affairs. Ha! Little did she know what a mess it all was.

"Who was your mother?" Aunt Camille said quietly, tears still caught in the back of her throat like she might cry at any moment.

"Ana Maria Quintana." Layla's voice had a funny catch to it as she added, "She died a couple years ago."

Aunt Camille's shoulders rose and fell. "I'm so sorry for your loss. My mother is right. Ana Maria was my friend. You must miss her terribly."

"I do," Layla said, a dark look crossing her face.

He knew that look. Felt the weight of it every day. Layla had lost someone very dear to her as well.

"You're welcome to keep the yearbook for as long as you like," Aunt Camille said. "I believe Ana Maria was involved in several activities, so there are probably several pictures of her. "I'd offer to make copies, but the printer here is broken."

Layla gave Aunt Camille a soft smile. "Thank you. My *abuela* has pictures, but I haven't seen these."

Once again, Andrew was struck by Layla's beauty and the way her smile lit up her eyes. A nurse dressed in scrubs with her hair pulled up didn't seem like society's view of an attractive woman, but he wouldn't mind spending more time looking at . . .

He shook his head. What was he thinking?

"What are we doing for therapy today?" Gram asked, her voice like a buzzer, changing the mood in the room.

"Um, therapy? Yes, of course." Layla cleared her throat and straightened. "As I was telling Andrew on the way in, we're going to do some meditation to help relieve the stress in this household. Did you know that meditation is something that even Jesus did?"

Having heard Andrew's objection, Layla must have

anticipated that Gram would be even more negative. Even though he still wasn't comfortable with Gram taking so much medicine, he appreciated how willing Layla was to adapt her treatment to Gram's needs. He liked the patient way she explained meditation, and how it was a spiritual practice, like prayer. While most people were impatient with Gram and her demanding questions and often surly attitude, Layla spoke to Gram with kindness and gentleness.

Aunt Camille stepped alongside Andrew. "I've never seen Mother so . . . open . . . before."

Andrew turned and looked at her. Could this be a way to make some of the conflict in their home ease up as well?

"Most people go at Gram like they're entering a fight. Layla treats her with respect."

For a moment, Aunt Camille looked like she was going to spout off one of her famous insults about how her mother didn't deserve respect, but then she nodded slowly.

"I guess we all treat her like the enemy, don't we?"

"We?" Andrew shook his head.

"You don't like me, either, do you?"

There was no anger in Aunt Camille's voice, and while it would have been easy enough to keep the peace and give the polite answer, he found he didn't have the energy to do so.

"Why should I? Until you and Caroline made up, you weren't nice to anyone in this house. And even now, when you're here, you start fights with Gram. You haven't tried getting to know me and Allie. It's like you have your own agenda, and the rest of us don't matter."

Aunt Camille pressed her lips together, as if she didn't like

Andrew's answer, but she'd asked so she couldn't really complain.

"You haven't tried getting to know me, either," she said.

He shrugged. "I was here first."

Strangely, Aunt Camille laughed. "I was born here, well before you were even a thought in your father's little brain."

Andrew chuckled at the idea of his father having a little brain. "Yeah, but you left."

A sad look crossed Aunt Camille's face. "But I'm here now. Doesn't that count for something?"

He glanced over at where Layla sat with Gram. "Maybe if you tried to work with her, to understand her needs, her desires, it would."

Then Gram caught his eye, jerking her head in a way to indicate she wanted him to join them. "I need to get over there. I promised I'd learn about meditation today."

Camille followed. Stopped in front of Gram. "Is it all right if I join you? I took a meditation class once, and I could use a refresher."

"It isn't one of those New Age things you love," Gram snapped.

"I know," Camille said, sitting next to Gram. "But maybe it's time I made the effort to learn about what you love, like I have with Caroline. I'm tired of being enemies."

He'd never seen such a surprised look on Gram's face.

Gram nodded, then looked over at Layla. "Do you charge extra for them to join in?"

Layla shook her head. "No. As Andrew and I discussed, reducing stress for everyone in the household will reduce stress for you, thereby lowering your blood pressure and keeping you off meds."

She smiled at him, looking slightly nervous, so he smiled back. He might not agree with everything she did, but he remembered reading in some of the cancer books he'd read when Mykel was sick that wellness was a journey for the whole family, and the greater the family commitment to wellness, the better chances of survival were. It wouldn't hurt to apply those principles to this situation.

"Then let's begin," Gram said, holding up one of the pamphlets Layla had given her. "I want to do this one on the Lord's Prayer. It's my favorite part of church, when we all say it together."

And so they began. As the familiar words rolled off Andrew's tongue and he did the breathing exercises Layla explained, he found that he did, in fact, feel some of the stress leave his body.

He could sense Layla near him, even though his eyes were closed, and he was trying not to be aware of her. She smelled like roses, not the fake perfume-y kind, but like what you'd find in Gram's garden. Somewhere in the back of his mind, in the place that always started to panic when he found himself aware of a woman, he felt a strange sense of peace, like everything was going to be all right.

Chapter Five

Something had changed in the Bigby household after their meditation session. Layla could only credit it to God working in all of their hearts as they prayed together and focused their thoughts on God instead of on all the worry and conflict. The past couple of weeks had been so peaceful, and much of the tension she'd sensed in the household had disappeared.

Andrew was still distant, but less guarded. Camille was starting to spend more therapy sessions with her mother, and Layla noticed that Enid was less critical of Camille. Layla had even met the elusive Allie. A rare feat, considering all the hours Allie worked. Her interactions with Caroline and Hayden had always been brief, but now, she felt more warmth from them.

Amazing how just a little understanding changed things.

As she packed her bag to head to the Bigby farm, her phone rang. Her boss.

"You haven't left for the Bigby place yet, have you?"

"No, why?"

"The old lady is in the hospital. I don't have all the details.

Andrew called to let us know, but he didn't give much information."

Layla stared at her phone. Why hadn't Andrew called her directly? She'd made sure they all had her numbers to keep her updated on Enid. After all the progress they'd made, it seemed odd that he wouldn't include her.

"Thanks."

Jack briefed her on a few other cases she'd need to look in on today, but Layla's thoughts remained on Enid. What had happened? Why hadn't they given Jack any details?

When they finally ended the call, Layla checked the clock. She'd have enough time to run by the hospital to check on the old woman before going on her rounds. She tried calling Andrew, but his phone went directly to voice mail. After leaving him a message, she sent him a text, hoping he'd answer with some information on his grandmother's condition.

The hospital wasn't far from her apartment, and when Layla got there, she could feel the anxiety rising. What if something bad had happened to Enid?

Before she let that thought take hold, she reminded herself to focus on God's word. But she couldn't get rid of the gnawing in her stomach.

"Hi Amy," Layla said, greeting one of the nurses as she entered the wing where Enid was most likely staying. "I hear one of my patients, Enid Bigby, is here."

Amy shook her head. "I'm not supposed to tell you anything." Then she looked around and said quietly, "Andrew is really upset and demanding a review of her medical care. If I were you, I'd make sure you've thoroughly documented everything, because if there is a dot missing from an 'i,' he's going to have your head."

That sounded like the Andrew she'd first met, not the Andrew of late. Layla took a deep breath. Something really bad must have happened.

"Who's the doc? You think he'd tell me anything? Enid's . . ." Layla tried not to get emotional. For all she'd done not to get attached to this family, to not get involved, it had happened anyway.

She took a moment to calm herself before continuing. "I know most people think she's an annoying old bird, but she's really grown on me, you know?"

Amy nodded. "I do. She doesn't like people knowing, but when Paul was late on child support again and I couldn't pay Lily's tuition for day camp, Enid let her come anyway. And when she overheard me at the store telling Lily we had to have ramen for dinner again because we were out of grocery money, I came home to find a basket of fresh vegetables and eggs on our porch. Life hasn't always been kind to her, but she's always given what she's able."

That sounded a lot like Enid and all the Bigbys.

"What about Andrew?" Layla couldn't help asking. Javier had hinted that he'd also had a rough past, but he'd refused to elaborate.

After looking around, Amy leaned in to Layla. "Do not pin your hopes on that one. One of the best guys you'll ever meet, but he is not on the market."

Layla sighed. "I've heard that a time or two. He's even given me his little speech. But why? And why is he being so difficult about letting me help his grandmother?"

This time, Amy let out a long sigh. "I forget that you aren't from here. You don't know the whole story. I go on break in fifteen minutes. Meet me in the staff lounge, and I'll tell you what I know."

"Thanks. See you in a few." Layla hated feeling like she was going behind Andrew's back, but none of this made any sense. She'd thought they'd come to a good place. So why was he shutting her out?

As she turned the corner towards the cafeteria to get a cup of coffee before meeting Amy, she saw Andrew pacing the hall.

"Andrew!" Layla dashed over to him.

He glared at her. "Go away. You've done enough damage."

"What do you mean by that?" She returned his glare. "You can't say something like that and expect me to just leave. How's Enid?"

"Alive, no thanks to you." He made a noise, then shook his head. "She had some kind of diabetic incident, and her blood sugar got too low. I found her passed out in the living room, so we called an ambulance and brought her here. They're doing tests, and they won't let me be with her."

Were it any other person, Layla would have reached out to him, squeezed his arm, or offered him some comfort. But he was so prickly, he'd probably find a way to call it assault or something.

"Has she been taking her meds?"

"Of course she's been taking her meds. That's probably what landed her in here. Stupid pharmaceutical companies. Getting rich off killing people."

It sounded like he was making a lot of crazy assumptions. Just like he had when they'd first discussed Enid's condition.

"So you don't know for sure what caused this?" Layla asked carefully.

"They said it was her blood sugar. I know that much. Those pills you had her taking-"

"Are not as effective as insulin in regulating blood sugar. This was an attempt at keeping her off insulin, but sometimes it's not enough. And her medications are not my decision, but her doctor's. If you're going to be mad at anyone for medication related problems, then you're accusing the wrong person."

She tried keeping her voice level, modulated, like the voice of reason, even though what she wanted to do was shake him for being so ignorant and bull-headed.

"But you talked her into them."

Layla couldn't help groaning. There was no reasoning with him. He needed someone to blame for Enid's condition, and since she was in front of him, he'd made her the target. So much for thinking they'd made progress with all the prayer and meditation.

"Maybe instead of being angry with me, and blaming me, you could be praying and asking for God's wisdom, both in how to handle the situation, and for the medical staff caring for your grandmother. It's hard to focus on giving good patient care when you have an angry relative breathing down your neck."

Not waiting for a response, Layla turned and continued down the corridor towards the cafeteria. Arguing with him wasn't going to solve anything, but maybe, just as God had already been working in their lives, He could help Andrew in a way she couldn't.

By the time she got her coffee, Amy was already in the break room, eating a salad out of a plastic container she'd probably brought from home.

"Thanks for being willing to talk to me," Layla said, joining her friend. "I ran into Andrew in the hallway, and he's so angry. There's a major chip on his shoulder, and I feel like it's bigger than just his grandmother being sick."

Amy nodded. "After college, he got a great job with a big company in Seattle. He was making tons of money. He had this fiancée who was beautiful, smart, and talented. I only met her once, briefly, but she was amazing. Everyone loved her. They were the quintessential perfect couple. Then they found out she had cancer. Andrew spared no expense in getting her treatment. At the doctor's urging, they gave her experimental drugs. It was supposed to be a miracle cure."

Layla's stomach twisted. She almost didn't need to hear the end of the story. "She died, didn't she?"

"On what was supposed to have been their wedding day," Amy said quietly.

A piece of Layla's heart shattered at Amy's words. Every broken look Andrew had given her suddenly made more sense than she could have imagined. "He thinks the drugs killed his fiancée, so he's afraid of any medicine, isn't he?"

"They weren't fully informed of all the risks and side effects. She should never have been on that drug. They pulled it from trials shortly after she died. When Andrew found out, he went a little crazy. His grandfather also died of cancer around the same time, so Andrew sold everything he owned, built a tiny house on the farm, and he's been there with his grandmother, wallowing in his grief, ever since."

Layla took a deep breath. "Please tell me Enid doesn't have cancer."

Shaking her head, Amy gave a small laugh. "Thankfully, no. I'm pretty sure that would send Andrew over the edge. Honestly, Enid's fine. She'll probably be released later today or tomorrow, depending on when her blood sugar stabilizes. She was feeling better, so she hasn't been taking her meds. Which sent her blood sugar out of control, and here we are. Once Andrew calms down, I'm sure you'll be tasked with educating her on the importance of always taking her meds, no matter how good she feels. I just couldn't say anything out there because of Andrew's rampage."

At least Enid would be all right. Clearly the old woman hadn't been paying attention to Layla's first lecture on taking her meds every day, no matter how she felt. But this would be a good illustration of why Layla had been so insistent.

"Thank you for telling me. I know I'm not supposed to get so attached, but . . ." Layla shrugged.

Amy smiled. "It's hard not to in such a small town. These people are our friends and our neighbors. We go to church with them, see them in the grocery store. It'd be a rough place to live if you didn't care."

Setting her fork down, Amy reached for Layla's hand. "And if it's any consolation, Enid was asking for you. Andrew won't be happy, but he's also not going to put up a fight since it's what she wants. She's in room 216. Go the back way so Andrew doesn't see you until it's too late."

"Thanks." Layla rose to leave, but Amy stopped her.

"But seriously, if you have any romantic thoughts about Andrew, give them up now. Something in him died when his fiancée died, and he hasn't been the same person. We all love the good, loving man he can be. But there's a deep anger and darkness in him that he refuses to heal. That's the side you're seeing right now. Everyone who cares about him has tried helping him, but he's successfully shoved everyone away. Andrew doesn't just burn bridges, he creates new gorges to rival anything the Snake River creates. It's not worth it. This battle is between him and God, and he doesn't let God in."

Layla stared at her friend for a moment. "But he seems to be such a man of faith."

Amy nodded. "He is. But we all have places we hide from God. Some more than others. In Andrew's case, it's a really big, deep place. With all he does for others he covers it well. But I think all the things he does are mostly to avoid facing the pain of his loss."

That sounded a lot like Andrew. And very neatly put together all the confusing pieces of the man she didn't understand. Though Amy gave sound advice in saying that Andrew was definitely not worth pursuing, Layla's heart was softening towards him in a deeper, more profound way.

**

Seeing Gram hooked up to all those wires and tubes made Andrew's heart hurt. The doctors were all saying she'd be fine, but would she? They all said the medicine would help her, but since she'd been taking the medicine, it seemed like she'd never been worse. She'd certainly never ended up in the hospital for low blood sugar before.

He shook his head. Maybe they needed to take Gram to a

better hospital. In a bigger town. Where there were experts who knew what they were doing. But that's what he'd done with Mykel, and now she was dead. So what was he supposed to do?

"Stop your pacing. You're making me dizzy," Gram said from her bed.

He dashed over to her side. "I didn't know you were awake. How are you feeling?"

She opened one eye. "How do you think I feel? I'm in a hospital. And I hear you're creating a ruckus."

Trust Gram to still know everything, even with being cooped up in that bed.

"I want to be sure they're doing right by you. I won't have another loved one killed by medicine."

Making an irritated noise, she opened her other eye. "I'm an old woman. You can't keep me alive forever."

"But you don't have to die because of a bunch of incompetent fools messing with your health."

The door opened and Layla walked in, flanked by Dr. Sloan. "Well, nice to know what you think of us," Layla said pleasantly, brushing past him to go to the other side of Gram's bed. "I hear you weren't taking your medicine."

"I felt fine, so I didn't think I needed it," Gram said, sounding like she'd been caught in the middle of making trouble.

"And what did I tell you about that?"

"She's not a child," Andrew answered for her. "Stop talking to her like one."

Layla looked up at him. "You are correct. She is a grown woman, and she's in here because of her bad choices. In this case, not taking medicine to regulate her blood sugar. Hopefully this has impressed upon her the importance of following doctor's orders."

"And what if the doctor's orders are wrong?" Andrew glared at her. What was Gram to Layla but just another name on a chart?

"You're free to get a second opinion. I'm sure the doctor can give you a list, or if you like, since it seems to be your preferred method of education, go ahead and look online. However, I don't think you're going to find anything different. Dr. Sloan is one of the best."

Dr. Sloan stepped forward. "Thanks, Layla."

Andrew watched as the doctor pulled out a piece of paper from his folder and stuck it to the wall.

"Here's a chart which shows the stability of your blood sugar based on the journal your grandmother was keeping," Dr. Sloan said, pointing to the bright lines of a graph. "As you can see, on the days that you took your meds when you're supposed to, your blood sugar remained relatively stable."

Then he pointed to another area of the chart with high peaks and low dips and points in between. "These are the days when you weren't taking your medicine at the right time."

Gram pushed the button to raise up on the bed, then folded her arms across her chest as she appeared to study the chart. "But I felt fine on those days. When I started feeling poorly, I would take a pill."

The doctor turned his attention to Gram. "And that's exactly what moved you from having the nice stable line, to having all the ups and down. You have to take the medicine at the prescribed times. Today, when you got too high, there wasn't enough time between taking the medicine and it getting into your system to keep you out of danger. We don't want to see those spikes because they're too hard on your body. Which is why you're here."

Andrew wasn't as impressed with the chart as Gram seemed to be. It was obvious that they'd made the chart specifically for her. Andrew knew how charts and data could be manipulated to tell whatever story the doctors wanted. Which meant this data was meaningless, and was probably just one more ploy to bully an old woman into treatment she didn't need.

"I just hate having to take all those pills," Gram said. "Why can't we get our nutrition from food?"

Layla stepped forward and rested her hand on Gram's arm. Like she was a friend who actually cared about his grandmother.

"Because sometimes, our bodies need a little extra help. You're doing a great job with good food. In fact, it's the reason why you haven't shown signs of diabetes until now. And, it's also why you can take this medicine rather than having to go on insulin. I'm sure you don't want to have to take a shot every day."

Gram nodded. "I do hate needles."

Andrew couldn't believe how easily they were persuading Gram to fall in line with what they wanted. She didn't know anything about these drugs. She didn't know the harm that they could cause her. They hadn't even discussed side effects.

"All the same, I'd like to get a second opinion." Andrew stared at Layla, challenging her.

"That's within your rights," Layla said. "But the longer you delay, the worse your grandmother's condition will become, and the harder it will be to keep her from having to do daily insulin shots. Your choice."

Andrew glared at her. "Your scare tactics don't work on me. I've heard them all. My grandmother is not going to be manipulated by fear."

Gram mumbled something, but Andrew couldn't hear her words. Layla did, and she reached forward and patted Gram's hand again. Maybe that would matter to some, but for Andrew, the gesture of kindness only served to make him feel more unsettled. How many doctors and nurses had done the same thing with Mykel? Pretending to be an ally, pretending to be her friend. All the while giving her a dangerous drug designed to kill her.

Layla said something to Gram that Andrew couldn't hear.

"What was that?" he asked. "Everyone thinks we're the ones unduly influencing elderly woman, but it seems to me you're doing just the same, keeping things from us."

"Let's talk outside," Layla said, coming back around the bed and taking Andrew by the arm. "Dr. Sloan will stay here with your grandmother. They have some things to discuss."

"You're not just trying to get rid of me to get her to make a decision without my input are you?"

Talk about elder abuse! He was here as Gram's advocate, and they were all trying to separate him from her.

Dr. Sloan shook his head. "Given that we all know how unhappy you are, and that you've threatened to sue us a number of times in the past hour, I would never do that." He pulled out his phone and held it up. "I've got some new pictures of my grandbabies, and I know Enid was eager to see them. So we'll be talking babies, and when you return, we can talk treatment."

Andrew still wasn't sure he could trust them, but something in the way Layla insisted on him going with her made him want to agree. No, that wasn't the right word. Compelled. He felt compelled to hear Layla out. Why she had such power over him, he didn't know, but it seemed like he couldn't say no. He was drawn to her and being forced to remind himself that she was the enemy.

"I know about your fiancée," Layla said quietly as she led him into a small conference room and closed the door. She touched his arm in that same familiar way she'd done with Gram.

He stared at her for a second, then shook her hand away. How could she bring up Mykel now? "Why is that relevant? My grandmother is ill, and you want to talk about something totally unrelated."

The look Layla gave him made him feel funny in his stomach. A warning that he wasn't going to like what she was going to say next. If it was anything about Mykel, he didn't need his stomach for that preview.

"I've been told that you're angry with doctors because of what happened with her and don't trust them."

"This is a waste of time," Andrew said. "My grandmother needs me, and you want to drag me out here to talk about a past that can't be changed? This is ridiculous."

Layla wanted to reduce his stress, did she? Clearly she had no idea how to go about it. He turned to leave, but Layla remained in front of the door. Not exactly blocking it, but enough to make him pause and stare at her.

She shook her head. "No, what's ridiculous is that you've stood in the way of your grandmother receiving quality care because of your unresolved grief issues. I don't know all the details, but I know your fiancée died, and I know you blame the doctors. That is a terrible thing to have to live with. I can understand how frightened you would be to see your grandmother unexplainably ill and feeling helpless because you don't understand what she's going through or what the doctors are trying to do. But right now, your grandmother isn't getting the quality of care she needs, and you're standing in the way."

Layla was blaming him for his grandmother's illness? Obviously this woman was off her rocker.

"You have no idea what I've been through. This has nothing to do with what happened. Except that I learned a lot about how the so-called experts work, and I learned not to blindly trust the doctors."

Though he could feel the pulse pounding in his head, Layla appeared completely unfazed. Calm. Like she'd been prepared for the damage she was doing by digging in to the private places of his heart.

"You're right that it's a good thing to do your due diligence," she said, her voice steady and gentle. "But let me ask you, what have you done to research your grandmother's condition, the drugs she's on, and alternatives? You continue to voice accusations, but you've given us no evidence, cited no studies, offered no viable solutions."

Andrew stared at her. He hated the questions. He had no answer. She was right. He'd taken a number of notes and done a few Internet searches, but he hadn't gotten far. He was so behind on all the farm work, so behind on all the things Caroline needed him to do, and he'd been trying to sit in on all of Gram's therapy sessions, which left little time to do research.

Layla continued to return his stare. Her expression scorched him to the bone, perhaps even deeper. She had him, and she knew it.

"Now let me tell you how this is going to work," she said. "You and I both know that your grandmother's case is still open. I can have her caseworker on the phone at any time."

And now she was resorting to threats. Threats she could carry out that might get Andrew off her back, but would probably ruin Gram's life. He and his cousins were Gram's only allies in protecting the way of life she so loved. But with Caroline so busy at the height of day-camp season, and Allie having so much on her plate, Andrew was the only one Gram had.

His stomach tightened as Layla continued.

"Your actions right now show that you're not acting in your grandmother's best interests. You're too consumed by your own grief and your own pain to think rationally about what's best for her. You've threatened the nursing staff so many times that they're all afraid to take care of your grandmother. But can you honestly tell me that anyone in this hospital has done anything to hurt her?"

Her words shamed him. Mostly because as he examined the question, he couldn't find one example where Gram had actually been mistreated. Though he had his doubts about the medication she was on, he couldn't say he knew for a fact that she didn't need it.

He sank into one of the chairs and put his head in his hands. What if he'd been too aggressive in how he'd been handling the situation? Had he put Gram in danger?

"So what am I supposed to do?" Andrew looked up at Layla, hating that she might be right.

She gave him a gentle look, but remained near the door. "I've talked to a counselor friend of mine, Helen McGrath. She has agreed to meet with you confidentially and help you work through your emotions. If you don't want to meet with her, that's fine. But understand that unless you can give me actual evidence that there is something potentially wrong with how Enid is being treated, your obstruction has to stop. You are endangering your grandmother's health by letting your grief blind you to the truth."

Andrew closed his eyes. Tried to think of a comeback or retort or something. If he didn't do what they wanted, they'd take over Gram's care and then . . . Andrew shook his head. He didn't want to even think about it. Basically they'd all gone from accusing his grandmother of being crazy to accusing him of being crazy.

"You're demanding that I get therapy?" He asked, making sure he understood exactly what they wanted.

"Someone has to."

Layla had the nerve to look sympathetic. Clearly all this caring was just an act. Just like it had been with Mykel's caregivers. But was it? Though he'd been mentally accusing Layla of being fake, he couldn't honestly say he believed it. He hated the way the doubts had started to creep into the back of his mind, making him unsure of just about everything.

With a kind smile, Layla said, "Sometimes the love and support of the family aren't enough to get beyond such a painful loss. But you have to find a way to deal with it, because your pain is making you irrational."

"I'm not crazy."

She took a step toward him, looking more relaxed, like she was no longer afraid he was going to bolt. "I'm not saying you are. I can't imagine how horrible it must have been to lose in such a painful way the woman you thought you were going to spend the rest of your life with. When my mother died of cancer, I thought the unbearable loss would drag me under. My father was no help, and none of my friends or other family understood what it was like to watch your mother die. Helen helped me. I think she can help you too."

Layla's words might have swayed another man, but part of Andrew wondered if this was just a ploy to get him to go along with treatment that would harm his grandmother. Wasn't that what they had done with Mykel? Spun dreams of seeing her walk down the aisle if only she'd give this new treatment another chance? He'd thought he was saving her life.

A knock sounded at the door, and Layla opened it, allowing a tall woman with dark hair and glasses to step inside.

"Andrew, this is Helen, the counselor I was telling you about."

"Hi Andrew. Is it okay if I join you?" Helen smiled at him, but Andrew couldn't muster the energy to do anything but nod.

Though Helen said something else, Andrew missed it. All he could think about was whether or not they were truly trying to help him, or if this was just one more tactic to get what they wanted.

But still, as he tried comparing Mykel's illness with Gram's, Andrew had to admit that nothing anyone did with Gram had given him doubts the way he'd had with Mykel's doctors.

He looked up at Layla, not bothering to blink away the tears that always filled his eyes when he was forced to speak about Mykel. "Did you know that it was an experimental drug, not the cancer, that killed her?"

It was all he could say. And the pain inside him that had been gnawing at his guts the entire time he'd been there at the hospital, reminding him of how hard it was to be in a hospital and why, made it almost impossible to breathe.

Helen said something to Layla, but Andrew couldn't hear, because there seemed to be a strange rushing in his ears. Layla nodded and stepped aside. Helen came and sat next to him. It was as though he was watching the whole experience as an outsider, not as a participant. Not as someone who should have been able to control things, who should have been able to say that he didn't want or need therapy, that he was just fine. But he couldn't do any of those things.

Andrew just sat. Then he blinked. And the rushing finally died down. Which Helen seemed to notice.

"I can see where that would be extremely painful," Helen said. "But not all medicines are experimental. From what Layla tells me, the medication your grandmother is on has been on the market for years and is well documented in helping patients with her condition. But I can see where you would be afraid. So let's talk about what happened to your fiancée. If you like, Layla can leave. What you say in here will be private. Just between us. But you've got to talk about it, and you need to help us understand, because otherwise you're putting your grandmother's life in danger."

Once more, those words taunted him. What if his grandmother's illness was his fault? Could he really be the reason why his grandmother was sick? What if he had been wrong in how he'd been handling the situation? He'd been wrong in how he handled Mykel's illness, blindly accepting the doctors' and nurses' decisions. But was he equally wrong in fighting them every step of the way with his grandmother?

Andrew closed his eyes and took a deep breath. Then he looked over at Layla. He'd been unfair to her, in a lot of ways. Especially if she had a sincere desire in her heart to help. Even in dragging him to this room. He'd said a lot of mean things to her, some of which he didn't feel like he could control. So maybe, if she knew the whole story, she would understand why he was so terribly broken, and why he was trying so hard to make sure no one hurt his gram.

"Layla can stay."

And then, in a final, broken plea, he begged God to help him understand the truth, and the right thing to do, because he wasn't sure he could live with himself if someone else he loved died because of his mistakes.

Chapter Six

The sun was shining, but it was a crisp morning as Layla walked into Abuela's house. It would be hotter later in the day, but she wished she'd brought a sweater. Abuela greeted her warmly with hug as she entered.

"Good morning," Layla said, smiling.

"So happy you are able to come by today." Abuela led her to the kitchen, which already smelled wonderful. "My friend Mona came by with some breakfast, and we're having some coffee while we wait for everyone."

Layla hesitated. She already felt bad for how she'd interfered with Andrew, finding out about his past, then forcing him to sit with the counselor. True, they'd made a great deal of progress in his counseling session. How would he feel when he learned she was meeting with his grandmother and her friends?

Even now, she wasn't sure what to do. Enid had been home a few days and was doing well. But Layla still hadn't figured out how to handle Andrew. Hearing Andrew's story, she understood why he would be so hesitant to believe the medical profession. His fiancée had a very curable form of cancer. She should have made it. But the doctors had convinced her to take an experimental drug, despite warnings and side effects. According to Andrew, he'd found that the symptoms she was having meant she should stop taking the drug, but his concerns were ignored by the medical staff, and his fiancée had died. Layla didn't understand why the doctors had made those choices, so she could understand his frustration. Andrew blamed himself for not digging deeper, for not doing more research, and for letting his fiancée continue to take those drugs. He'd wanted to believe so badly in a miracle, that he had let the doctors talk them into treatment that had ultimately harmed her.

So now here they were, fighting over his grandmother's treatment. Though Enid was home and doing well, Layla was dreading going over there and running into Andrew. Though he'd let her sit in on his session, afterward, he'd made it clear that he wanted nothing to do with her. He resented her interference and was angry that she'd gone behind his back. In some ways, rightfully so. But she'd needed answers as to why he was so opposed to his grandmother's care, when everything was standard practice and routine.

Which was why she had a bad feeling about being here.

"It's so nice to meet you," Mona said. "You've made your grandmother's heart full by coming back into her life. I don't think people realize how hard it is for an old woman facing the end of her life to look at her family with pride and yet have a hole in her heart for missing family members."

Layla smiled. "Abuela's not going anywhere any time soon."

Mona held up a coffee cup. "Only the Lord knows the number of our days, and we must make the most of however

Greene County Library
120 N. 12th St.
Paragould, AR 72450

many we have. So it's good that you're finally here while we still have time. Coffee?"

"Please. And now I know why you're friends with Enid. You sound just like her."

Mona grinned as she filled the coffee cup. "We both grew up together. Raised our families together. Buried our husbands together. I suppose that makes us of similar mind at times. We also have our differences, and I do think sometimes she is just a little too stubborn for her own good."

Abuela laughed. Then pointed to Mona's arm that was in a cast. "Says the woman who broke her arm riding one of those crazy motorcycles. You're 80 years old. What were you thinking doing a foolish thing like that?"

Mona shrugged. "I always wanted to try it. And I did. I'm not going to my grave wishing I tried something. I'm doing it all."

Abuela shook her head. "And you want me to join that nutty granny group of yours?"

Layla had heard about the grannies. They were a group of octogenarians or close to it, who did all sorts of wild and crazy things for the fun of it. On one hand, Layla could respect the desire to get the most out of life and live it to its fullest, doing everything you always wanted to do without fear. On the other hand, some of their antics were borderline stupid.

"Just don't get yourself killed, Abuela," Layla said, smiling.

"Not a chance. They're going zip lining by the Snake next weekend. I don't even know what that is."

Mona launched into a discussion about zip lining, and how there was a tour company near the Snake River. According to the brochure, it was a great way to see the countryside, and even though it was probably fine for most adults, Layla could see where it was a good way for a bunch of elderly ladies who didn't have the strength and dexterity of people fifty years their junior to get themselves killed.

"Is this why you brought me here? Am I supposed to be talking you into this endeavor or out of it?" Layla smiled at Mona then winked at her grandmother.

Mona cackled and pounded the table. "I like this granddaughter of yours. She's got spirit and spunk, just like her mother did."

"That she does," Abuela said. "Sometimes it makes my heart hurt seeing so much of my Ana Maria in her. I only wish I could've told my daughter how much I loved her before she died."

They hadn't really spoken of this. Usually Abuela avoided all references to Layla's mother.

"Then why didn't you?" Layla asked, unable to help herself.

Abuela sighed and sank back into her chair. "Because it caused too many problems with your father. He wants to be American in every way, and while I understand that, because I believe in embracing a new country and its customs, I also want to hold on to some of the old traditions to preserve them for future generations."

The older woman looked sad as she spoke, and Abuela didn't need to elaborate, because Layla understood all too well. Any time she'd tried to do anything to explore Mexican culture, her father had gotten angry. He called her mother's family a lot of bad names, and hated that they were preserving their traditions.

Layla went over to her grandmother and gave her a big hug.

"I'm sorry if I sounded accusatory. I didn't mean to hurt you. I've just never understood the breach in our family, and I've never understood my father's hostility."

Abuela shrugged. "It doesn't matter now. What matters is that you're here, and we're all together. I pray your father will someday come around, and he will see that one can be an American and Mexican, and proud to be both."

Mona set cups of coffee in front of them, then gave them each a plate with steaming quiche and a warm cinnamon roll.

"Now I feel bad for not making something Mexican," she said, grinning. "But everyone says they love my quiche and cinnamon rolls, and I don't cook Mexican as well as your *abuela* does. But I hope you'll enjoy this."

Layla returned the smile. "I'm sure I will. Any meal I don't cook is a good meal."

Mona banged on the table again. "We need to get down to business. We had prayer group last night, and Enid told us she has diabetes. I know it was hard for her to talk about because she lives such a healthy lifestyle, but it's like I told her, sometimes, you do everything right, and you still get sick. That's just life. She asked us for help. And that's what we're here to do."

Now that was something unexpected. It also relieved some of the stress Layla felt at being there. Less like she was going behind anyone's back.

"Really? That's good to hear. She needs the support of her friends, especially if she's not getting the support she needs from family."

Mona made a noise. "That Andrew. He always did have a flair for the dramatic. I know everyone says he's the sensible one,

70

but I think he balances it out with his own share of drama. You should've seen him in the school plays."

Mona shook her head, and turned to Abuela. "Do you remember when he and Javier played best friends in *Hamlet*?"

Abuela laughed. "They were so good. I always did think Javier should have been a movie star. But with Alex becoming a baseball star, I'm glad he didn't. Sometimes being a star creates more headache than it's worth."

The back door opened, and Enid walked in.

"I'm starting to think that Andrew has been brainwashed by the Communists. Do you know that he would not let me leave the house? I had to bribe Camille to bring me over. And we still had to sneak out. Me, at my age, sneaking out of my own home. Andrew is out of control."

She went over to the table and dished herself out a helping of the quiche, then paused at the cinnamon rolls, and looked at Layla. "I suppose I'm not allowed to have this, am I?"

Before Layla could answer, Mona put a cinnamon roll on Enid's plate.

"Yes, you can. I got this recipe from a diabetic cookbook. It's specially formulated to help people still be able to enjoy sweets, but not have to worry about a spike in blood sugar."

Something about the older woman's gesture brought tears to Layla's eyes. This was the kind of support she'd hoped to find by moving to a town like Arcadia Valley.

If only she could figure out a way to get Andrew in on the support bandwagon.

**

Andrew pounded the steering wheel of his truck as it sputtered to a halt in front of Arcadia Valley Community Church. The gas gauge wasn't working properly, which was why he always kept careful track of his gas. Allie had borrowed his truck yesterday to help a friend, and she'd promised to fill the tank. Clearly, she hadn't.

He let out a long sigh. It was just the way this crummy day was going, he supposed. He'd caught Gram trying to go out in her car, when she knew she wasn't cleared to be driving with her injured leg. When he'd finally gotten her back into the house and reasonably calmed down, and gotten back to working on the tractor that he still couldn't figure out, he'd seen Camille's car pulling away, with Gram leaning out the window, yelling, "Take that, you Commie!"

Clearly everyone thought he was the bad guy.

And maybe he was. He knew, especially after his counseling session, he'd overreacted to Gram having to go to the hospital for her diabetes. But what was he supposed to do when the fear overtook him like that? Yes, he knew Gram wouldn't live forever. But he wasn't ready to say goodbye to her yet.

Andrew got out of the truck and headed up the walk to the church. Maybe the pastor had a gas can he could borrow. He usually kept one in the back of his truck, but it was oddly missing.

"Andrew!" Pastor Harris greeted him as he entered. "Funny to have you come by, I was going to pay you a visit this afternoon."

Andrew tried not to groan. He knew Gram had gone to her prayer group the previous night, and with the way she'd called him a Commie this morning, he had a pretty good idea that she'd

THE THOUGHT OF ROMANCE

probably asked the pastor to come have a word with him. He suddenly felt like a little kid, about to get the lecture of a lifetime.

"No need to look worried," Pastor Harris said, putting an arm around him and gesturing to his office. "Do you have time for a cup of coffee?"

Considering he had no idea where Camille had taken Gram, and he wasn't looking forward to driving in to Twin Falls for another tractor part, he supposed he had worse options in life.

"Sure, why not?" He tried not to sound resigned, but the pastor patted him on the back.

"You've had a rough time of things lately, haven't you?"

Andrew didn't answer. It seemed like everyone wanted to talk to him about his feelings and analyze his life. He'd gotten his fill of it from Layla, that was for sure. He still couldn't believe she'd railroaded him into seeing a shrink.

Whose card was burning a hole in his shirt pocket.

"I noticed you haven't been to men's group lately. We miss you."

Andrew let out a long sigh. Javier had been asking him to come back, but it seemed like too many things got in the way.

"I've been busy."

Pastor Harris nodded. "I understand the day camp is at capacity again."

"And Allie's been working a lot lately, and Gram's been sick, and there just doesn't seem to be enough hours in the day. I have no idea what we're going to do when it comes time to harvest all the lavender."

Especially with a broken tractor. "You wouldn't happen to know anyone who's good at figuring out tractors, would you?

I've asked everyone I know, but none of them can figure out why it's not working."

With a smile, Pastor Harris handed him a cup of coffee. "There's cream and sugar on the counter if you want some."

"I like it black, thanks." Andrew took a sip, trying to get his racing thoughts to slow down for a change. Layla's suggestion of meditating on Bible verses popped into his mind. Why did she have to come into their lives and mess up a perfectly good routine? He'd been just fine until she'd arrived. Gram had been fine. Everything had been . . .

Andrew closed his eyes. Maybe it hadn't been fine. But it was working well enough.

"You really are exhausted, aren't you?"

Pastor Harris's voice interrupted his thoughts, and Andrew opened his eyes with a start.

"I'm sorry, I didn't mean to be rude. I was just thinking about everything."

"Tell me what's going on. I know things have been a struggle, and that's why I was going to come by later. To see what we can do to help."

Before Andrew could answer, the office door opened, and Mona entered, flanked by Javier's grandmother, Layla, and Gram. At least that was one more mystery solved.

"I didn't know you had someone here," Mona said, smiling. "We've come to discuss a new support group we're forming."

Gram stepped forward. "It's for people with diabetes. Layla says that we can all benefit from sharing knowledge, recipes, and just talking about how diabetes affects us. I didn't know I could eat healthy and still get diabetes."

Pastor Harris looked over at Andrew like Andrew had something to do with this. Andrew shrugged. This was all news to him.

Even though Layla was on the other side of the room, Andrew could feel her presence, almost as though she was standing next to him. He wasn't sure if he wanted to hug her or shake her. Everything in his life was topsy-turvy thanks to her, and he wasn't sure he liked it.

Mostly, though, he hated the emotions rising in him.

What had she done to him?

"I'm sure that would be of great benefit to our congregation," Pastor Harris said. "I also have diabetes, and while it's under control, Janet is always looking for new recipes to support our healthy lifestyle."

Gram nodded. "And Layla is going to teach us meditation. Did you know that meditation can lower your blood pressure naturally? I thought meditation was a weird thing from some other religion, but Layla has taught me to meditate on the Bible. Even Andrew has joined us."

At least she wasn't calling him a Commie in front of the pastor. But the glare she shot Andrew told him she was still mad at him. Some days, he felt like their roles had been reversed.

"It's true," Andrew said. "It's been good to think about God's word as an alternative to worry, even though I haven't been doing a good job of it."

The weight of Layla's gaze on him made him feel even worse. When it came to her, he hadn't done a good job of much of anything, especially in how he treated her. He knew he owed her yet another apology, and though the words were not hard to come by, he wasn't ready to deal with the emotions she stirred up in him.

This wasn't just about a basic human interaction, but the fact that he felt something deeper for her. Feelings he wasn't ready to examine. Not when he was still in love with Mykel.

The pastor nodded slowly. "I recently attended a seminar on the Bible as a meditation tool. I found it quite interesting, even though I haven't yet had time to put it into practice. Perhaps, instead of limiting the group to just diabetics, we could call it a healthy living group, and people with blood pressure problems, or other health problems, or those who are just interested in being more healthy, could join us for tips and support on living healthier lives."

"I like how you think," Mona said. "I heard there are some great Christian diet and exercise books out there. We tried reading one for our book club once, but then we decided to go fishing instead."

Andrew tried not to laugh at Mona's explanation for the book club. The ladies had tried reading a number of books as part of their granny group, but they usually stopped reading the book midway because it inspired them to do some other activity. As long as it didn't involve them stealing his tractor for tractor races again, he usually didn't mind.

"It's a great idea," the pastor said. "I'm assuming you ladies will take charge of this group? You'll have to check with the church secretary to see when we have open space, but I'm interested to see what you all do with it."

A wide grin filled Gram's face. It had been a long time since he'd seen her smile like that.

"Good. I already spoke with Shirley, and she said we can use the community room. Our first meeting is tomorrow. Layla's therapist friend is going to come and talk about how managing our emotions is good for our health. And next Saturday, we're having an all-day seminar on how to live a healthy lifestyle that glorifies God as we care for the bodies He gave us. We'll be having seminars once a month, so mark it on your calendar."

Gram looked straight at him as she spoke, and Andrew couldn't help thinking she'd somehow finagled this whole situation to teach him a lesson.

"Andrew, since you won't let me drive, you'll just have to come too."

Shaking his head, he looked over at Layla. "You created this monster. Why don't you explain to her that she's not yet cleared to drive, so she can stop being mad at me?"

Layla just grinned. "I could, but it's kind of fun watching you squirm."

If only she knew. He hadn't stopped squirming since the moment he met her.

Chapter Seven

Andrew had to admit the health group his grandmother and her cronies had formed wasn't all that bad. At least they had good snacks. He bit into one of the muffins the folks from the new bakery in town had brought and was pleasantly surprised to notice that for something that was supposedly healthy, it was delicious.

They were taking a short snack break, and then they'd be splitting off into smaller groups to discuss specific issues affecting their health. Whatever that meant. Andrew was as healthy as a horse. Never sick. And despite all of Layla's talk about blood pressure, his was fine. But at least it meant he wouldn't have her sitting near him. That woman was distraction personified. Every movement, every sound, every little thing she did drew his attention. And the perfume she was wearing . . . whatever it was called, it should be banned.

Who wanted to smell like roses, anyway?

Layla approached, carrying a stack of papers. "Did you get one? It's a self-assessment for your emotional health. You'll be going over it in your group."

He didn't answer. They'd barely spoken since she'd forced him into that counseling session, and he still didn't know what to say to her. Thanks for bringing back the nightmares he'd thought he'd successfully banished?

Sorry he'd been such a jerk? Those words were the ones on his lips the most. She'd sat in on his counseling session and knew his fears about doctors and medicine, so she probably understood and would be gracious. Still, it seemed easier to keep her at a distance. There was something else between them, something deeper and more personal, and the thought of opening up to that . . .

Andrew shook his head. He didn't want to talk about that stuff any more than he had to.

"I know this is difficult for you," she said slowly. "But I hope you'll give it an honest effort. It would really mean a lot to your grandmother for you to . . . heal."

The last word was almost like it had been something she'd been afraid to say. Everyone danced around that idea, probably because they knew that it wasn't possible to simply move on when the best part of your life had been shattered. Still, everything she said was like a taunt.

"Are you accusing me of being dishonest?" He snatched the paper out of her hands and glanced at it. None of the questions meant anything to him, but she seemed to think they would.

"Of course not. I just meant . . ." Layla let out a long sigh. "Can we step outside for a moment? I promise your virtue will remain intact, but if we don't clear the air between us—"

She shook her head. "We just need to make things right, okay?"

The last thing Andrew wanted was to be alone with Layla.

But she seemed genuinely distressed, and even though he had no intention of ever being her friend, deep down, he didn't want to be her enemy either.

"All right."

He led her out to the small courtyard on the side of the church. Though it was out in the open and anyone could see them out the community room windows, they would have enough privacy to talk.

Layla sat on a bench and patted the spot next to her, but Andrew chose another bench across from her.

He thought he spied an annoyed look cross her face, but he forced himself to ignore it. Being close to her meant she might touch him, and when she touched him, he felt things he didn't like to feel.

"I'm sorry for blindsiding you with Helen and forcing you into a counseling session. I just didn't know what else to do," Layla said, looking at him like she truly regretted her actions. "I don't know how to make you understand that the situation with your fiancée is nothing like what your grandmother is going through. She needs your love and support, but it seems like everything just makes you angrier."

Layla let out a long breath. "When we first met, you accused me of not listening to your grandmother and pursuing my own agenda for her health. I suppose I've been doing that to you as well. I apologize for not taking the time to hear you. So I'm here. Listening. What do you need to come to an emotionally healthy place so you can be an ally to your grandmother?"

Her voice caught, like it had been hard for her to admit where she'd gone wrong.

Maybe that was the problem. They'd both gone wrong in so many ways, and fixing it seemed almost impossible.

"I just need to be left alone," he said, his chest knotting so tight it was hard to breathe.

He hated that feeling. But it seemed to consume him these days, especially when people like Layla wanted him to talk about his grief.

"But that doesn't help anyone. How do you heal if you won't face it?"

Andrew closed his eyes. "I don't want to face it. I want to bury myself in the work, where it doesn't hurt anymore. Where I'm too busy to think about Mykel, and how none of my dreams will ever come true."

"None?"

Even with his eyes closed, he could tell Layla had shifted on the bench, coming closer to him. She would touch his hand, or his arm, something to offer him comfort, and he wasn't sure he could stand it. But part of him craved it.

"You can make new dreams," she said. "What about saving the farm from your other family members? Isn't that a dream worth fighting for? And your grandmother. Wouldn't having her back to her old antics on the farm be a dream come true?"

He opened his eyes and looked at her. "But I'll still be alone."

The tender look on her face nearly undid him. He shouldn't have been so honest, but something about Layla provoked it in him.

"You don't have to be," she said, taking his hand. "But that's your choice. You're the one pushing everyone away."

Layla squeezed his hand, and it would be so easy to squeeze

back. But he couldn't. She squeezed again, and Andrew thought the burning in his chest would kill him for sure.

"I can't get involved with anyone else," he said, looking her in the eye.

"No one's asking you to. But there is a whole community of people who love you, and you're missing out on so much because you've buried yourself. You've been given the gift of life, and you're not using it because you're having a major hissy fit that your fiancée was taken from you too soon. Guess what? None of us have a guarantee of tomorrow. So why are you acting like you're already dead instead of taking advantage of the time you have?"

He pulled his hand away and stood, turning his back to her. He'd been to therapy before she'd dragged him in to see Helen. The therapist had said essentially the same thing.

Though being accused of having a hissy fit was a new one.

Andrew tossed that idea around in his mind. He should be mad at the insult, except like most of the things Layla accused him of, she was right.

Truth time? Fine.

He turned and looked at her. "Because I lived like that once. And having it taken away, watching the woman I love die, it was too much to bear. Sure. I could build a new life, probably do a lot of wonderful things. And what then? It could be taken from me in an instant, and I refuse to go through that again."

Just as most of their painful conversations ended, Andrew shook his head as he walked away. He'd have liked to have gone all the way home, but Gram would need a ride. So he went back into the church, doing his best to stuff the feelings back in and sew the gaping wound shut.

He passed Javier on the way in, but he couldn't bring himself to greet his friend. Javier knew him too well, and Andrew wasn't sure he could hold it together after being completely gutted by Layla.

**

When Andrew left, Javier joined Layla on the bench. "What was that about?"

Layla sighed. She'd pushed Andrew too hard once again. "Me, trying to fix something that's none of my business."

"What did you do to him?"

"Pushed too hard I guess. I know I should go and slowly and gently, for whatever reason there's something about the two of us when we're together that ends up being explosive."

Javier shook his head. "Don't go there. You'll only be hurt in the end."

"What's that supposed to mean? I'm just trying to help him. Is that so wrong?"

Javier looked at her like she had no brains at all. "I see the way you look at him. From what the ladies all say, Andrew is a good-looking guy. He's smart, funny, and if all the giggling women who've chased after him over the years are to be believed, he's everything a woman wants. Except he's unavailable."

Layla couldn't help sighing again. She'd heard this before, a million times, from just about everyone who knew them both. "I know."

There was no sympathy on Javier's face. "No, you don't. Deep down, you're hoping to fix him. You're hoping that under your tender loving care, he's going to wake up and realize what a fool he's been for hiding behind his grief all these years. Let me give away the ending. It's not going to happen. Leave him alone. Go find yourself a nice guy who will appreciate you and wants your help. Andrew would never mean to, but he's only going to break your heart."

Layla stared at him. "You barely know me. You don't know how things are going to go. You don't even know my intentions."

Javier chuckled. "Oh but I do. You forget that I've known Andrew his whole life. I've seen the girls chasing him since junior high. Guess how many he dated?"

Layla shrugged, trying to picture him dating a bunch of girls. Somehow, she couldn't conjure up an image of Andrew on a date.

"None. You know who he took to prom? One of the handicapped kids. He overhead the cheerleaders making fun of her, saying she'd never get a date. So he took her to prom, and then sat with her every lunch because no one else would. He made it clear they were just friends, and that no one should be treated like those girls treated her."

A thoughtful look filled Javier's face. "I had the same girlfriend through high school, so I was never out looking. But I know how all the girls plotted and conspired, hoping they'd figure out a way to catch Andrew. All of Molly's friends at one time or another tried getting us to fix them up with Andrew on a double date. It never worked. He's always been happy enough on his own."

Now *that* she could picture. Even now, with how standoffish Andrew was, she'd seen the way some of the single women at church looked at him. But he seemed oblivious.

Or maybe not. She'd noticed when a few of the braver single women brought him his favorite baked goods, he'd always politely thanked them, then left them at the coffee station for everyone in the congregation to enjoy. Was that what he thought of her? That she was like one of them, throwing herself at him? Clearly Javier did.

And all right, so she would like to see him find healing. But not just for herself.

"He needs to get over his anger, because it's hurting his grandmother."

Javier shook his head. "You and I both know that he's never going to get over it until he decides to do it for himself."

"But something has to motivate him to start the process," Layla said, trying to tamp down her rising frustration.

"Do you honestly think you're the only one who wants to help him? When Andrew first came back we all tried in our own way to get him to sort through his grief. Me, our men's group, the pastor, and some of his other friends. It is easier for him to sit in his pain than to dream again."

Layla nodded. "That's pretty much what he said. He didn't want to chase after a new dream that could be taken from him at any moment."

"And that's why he will never fall in love with you," Javier said. "Please give up any romantic ideas you might have about him. Don't let your heart set itself on a man who will never love you the way you deserve to be loved. I saw how he loved his fiancée. It consumed him. Sometimes I think that completely burned out his love tank, and there's nothing inside him to fuel a romantic relationship with anyone else."

Giving her a sympathetic look, Javier continued. "I should know. After Molly and I broke up, no one else came close to comparing to her. I'd built up this standard that was so big, no other woman could compete. I have a feeling Andrew is doing the same thing. You'll never be able to compete with Mykel's memory."

While Layla would have liked to believe her cousin's words, it went against the fact that she always believed that a person's capacity to love was limitless. Maybe you thought you would never be able to love another person again, but it didn't mean you couldn't.

Javier stood, then bent to give her a quick hug. "I hope you know I'm saying this out of love, for both of you. Andrew is a great guy, and I'd love to see him find the same happiness I have. But you deserve better than playing second fiddle to a dead woman."

He turned in the direction of the church, then looked back at her. "I think they're starting up again. Don't get caught out here brooding, it won't do you any good. I'd better get back in there. Molly's giving a presentation on how even our most beloved unhealthy foods can be made healthy."

He meant well, and Layla appreciated the fact that her cousin looked out for her. She'd always longed to have family to guide her in her life. Maybe she should listen to Javier. There had been no one to warn her about Troy, another man she thought she could fix. She loved him deeply. But he'd loved his drug habit more. Layla had thought that if she just supported him enough, encouraged him enough, and given him a reason to live bigger than the drugs, that he'd eventually get better.

He hadn't.

True, he'd overdosed after they broke up, but Layla had always wondered if she'd just fought a little harder, then maybe she would have been able to save him.

Troy used to tell her no one could save him.

She hadn't believed him, just as she didn't want to believe Andrew. But maybe she should.

Chapter Eight

Andrew paused on his way to the room where the men were supposed to meet. They were setting up in the sanctuary for a funeral later that day. Some old lady he didn't really know, but Gram probably did.

Along the wall, someone had created a series of poster boards where members of the church had written tributes to her as comfort to the family. A lot of the usual stuff, like, *she was a nice lady. She'll be missed.* What struck him the most, however, was one of the notes someone had written. *At least she's back with her beloved Norman again.*

No offense to the person who'd written it, but when Mykel died, Andrew hadn't found those comments very helpful. Actually, he'd thought them quite idiotic. She might be in heaven, but what was he supposed to do in the meantime while he waited to go there?

He hated how everyone acted like they knew and thought that it would somehow provide comfort. Maybe it would comfort the family of the woman who'd died, or maybe it wouldn't. It just frustrated him to see how everyone acted like they had all the answers when really no one knew anything about anything at all.

Like moving on with his life. That's what everyone wanted him to do. But how could he, when everything he'd ever wanted was to do everything with Mykel?

Layla had accused him of burying himself. She was probably right. He didn't enjoy many things these days, but if he said it out loud, they'd probably lock him up for being suicidal. It wasn't that he was actively trying to die, he just didn't much feel like living was worth anything.

A little girl, maybe about nine or ten years old, came up to him. "Did you know my Nana?"

Great. A grieving family member. Exactly the thing he didn't need right then.

"I'm sorry, no," he said. Then he pointed to one of the pictures someone had tacked to the board. "But she seems like she was a lovely person. I'm sorry for your loss."

The little girl sighed. "Everyone says that. They're sorry for my loss. Why are they sorry? They didn't give Nana the cancer. It's not their fault she died."

Her innocent question made him smile. After all, hadn't he asked the same kinds of questions? Hearing it from a child, though, made him stop and think. Gave him a safe place to process what people had said when Mykel died.

He turned to child. "I think, when people say they're sorry, it means they have sympathy for you. They know you're sad, and they wish you weren't sad, but they understand."

Remembering the somber faces at Mykel's funeral, he added, "Most people know what it's like to lose someone they love, so they're also trying to express that they've felt similarly, even if they don't fully know the depths of your sadness."

As he spoke, he realized just how unkind he'd been to his friends and family who'd only been trying to share in his sadness, to give him support the best they knew how. He'd angrily brushed them aside because they couldn't possibly know. Except Gram, and she'd given sympathy in a different way.

She looked up at him. "Did you lose someone you love?"

Andrew nodded. "My fiancée. She had cancer too."

Tears filled the little girl's eyes. "My mom says that cancer is no one's fault, and that sometimes it's just a person's time. But why would God take away someone so wonderful and give them something as horrible as cancer?"

All questions he'd angrily asked God. Sometimes, he thought he still might be mad at God, because the answers to those questions seemed so arbitrary and unfair.

"I don't know." Andrew spied a nearby set of chairs. "You want to go sit?"

Looking hesitant, the little girl shrugged. "My mom says I shouldn't talk to strangers, but you're the only person who hasn't patted me on the head and told me it's going to be all right. How can it be all right when my Nana is gone?"

Tears streamed down the little girl's face, and Andrew couldn't help kneeling and taking her into his arms. She sobbed against his shoulder, and he let her cry, not caring that she was getting his shirt all wet. This poor child had lost so much and was trying to bravely face a world that didn't make sense without her nana.

He knew what that was like. Not losing a grandmother, thank

God, but losing the rudder which kept him on a course that made sense. Andrew felt the tears flow from his own eyes, and unlike most of the time, when he quickly brushed them aside and pretended it was all right, he let himself cry. For his loss. For this child's loss. And for all the losses that made no sense at all.

She looked up at him, her face red, tears still flowing, and her nose dripping with snot. Andrew smiled in spite of the situation. He probably looked just as awful.

"Why are you crying?"

He took a deep breath. "I may not know what it's like to lose a beloved grandmother, but you reminded me of how sad I am that my fiancée died. We're not always allowed to cry when we need to, but I want you to know that if you ever need to cry, you come to me, and I'll let you cry."

"Does this make us friends?" The little girl looked up at him hopefully. He remembered that she'd just informed him that he was a stranger and she shouldn't be talking to him. He probably shouldn't have been so encouraging to her, since he technically was a stranger, but it seemed almost second nature to comfort a child. Especially since he'd spent so much time helping with the day camp and children's ministry here at church. Actually, if he thought about it, he might even know the child.

"It does," he said, smiling. "I'm Andrew Bigby, and I'm proud to call you my friend. What's your name?"

With a shy smile, the little girl said, "McKenna Stone. My Nana was Nellie Lowell."

Nellie Lowell. Now Andrew remembered. She had been one of Gram's friends, one of the grannies, in fact. Gram was probably planning on attending the funeral later today, but had neglected to mention it since they'd already be here at the church.

"Nellie was a good friend of my Gram's. She made the best molasses cookies. She used to give me some when I came to mow her lawn as a teenager."

Andrew hadn't gone by Nellie's in years. Not since coming back to Arcadia Valley after Mykel's death. He'd avoided most everyone he used to know. Just the die-hards who wouldn't give up on him.

"So you did know my Nana." McKenna smiled, her face lighting up at the positive memory Andrew had shared.

"It's been a while since I've talked to her, but yes, I knew her. I guess that makes us not strangers after all."

McKenna nodded. "And we know the Bigbys! I was going to go to day camp next month, but we needed the money to pay for the funeral, so I can't go now."

Her face darkened, but then lightened up again. "But maybe when I do get to go, I can come say hi to you."

There was some good Andrew could do here. That, at least, was a positive thing he could do to help a sad little girl. It wouldn't replace her beloved grandmother, but maybe it would bring some joy to her life.

"I'll tell you what. As long as your parents agree, you can still come to camp. No charge."

McKenna let out a long sigh. "My parents are divorced. It's just me, my mom, and my older brother. Josh babysits me while Mom works, but he's so mean. I'm sure my mom will say yes."

Caroline was going to kill him for this, but how many extra kids had she taken in and made him figure out a way to make it work?

"You're welcome at Bigby Farm at any time. And if there's no room in the camp, you can come be my assistant. Have you ever worked on a tractor?"

McKenna's eyes lit up. "For real? I don't know how to work on them, but I could learn. If it means I get to ride on a real tractor."

They usually didn't let the campers on any of the farm equipment for safety reasons, but he'd find a way to make it legal for McKenna to do so. He'd probably have to get her mom to sign a million waivers, but it would be worth it to help this kid.

"As long as it's all right with your mom."

A woman came around the corner and smiled at them. "As long as what's all right with your mom?"

It took a moment, but Andrew recognized Sarah Lowell, now Stone. Or maybe it was back to Lowell. She was older than he was, but he remembered she used to babysit him and Allie when they were little.

"Hi Sarah, Andrew Bigby. I don't know if you remember me or not."

"Of course!" Sarah stepped forward and gave him a big hug. "You used to set your sister's dolls on fire."

Ouch. Bad memory to lead with.

He scratched his head. "Uh, the fires were an accident. Collateral damage of trying to send dolls to space on the rockets I built with my dad and my friends."

Sarah smiled. "If you say so. It's nice to see you again." Then she turned to McKenna and held out her hand. "Come on, Kens. Nana's viewing is about to start."

The viewing. Andrew swallowed. The thing where they dress

93

up a dead body and everyone gawks at it, pretending the shell of the human being looks remotely like the person did while alive. Mykel had weighed ninety pounds when she'd died. No amount of makeup could turn her back into the vibrant woman she'd once been. Andrew had taken one look at the fake, dressed up body and puked.

"I don't want to," McKenna said, looking nervous. "That's not my Nana."

Giving an impatient huff, Sarah said, "We've been through this. Let's go."

McKenna didn't move. Andrew took a step back towards Sarah. "If it's all right with you, McKenna can just hang out with me. We were talking about how hard it was to lose someone you love, and, well, we all deal with grief differently. I can relate to how she feels because I went through something similar when my fiancée died."

Sympathy lined Sarah's face. If she'd been back in Arcadia Valley for long, she probably knew the whole story like everyone else.

"Yes, of course. I remember." Then she looked over at McKenna. "Are you sure you don't want to come to the viewing? It's your last chance to say goodbye in private."

McKenna looked up at Andrew. He knew exactly what she was thinking. How did you say goodbye to a body that was already dead? When you had a million things you still wanted to say but would never get to. Her nana wasn't in that casket, and it wasn't going to make her feel any better to pretend otherwise.

"I'm sure," McKenna said. "Andrew doesn't treat me like I'm a stupid kid. I want to stay with him."

Sarah hesitated. "I don't want to be any trouble."

"Not at all. To tell the truth, being able to comfort your daughter has given me comfort. I'd be honored to support her in any way I can."

"You're positive?"

Andrew nodded.

Tears filled Sarah's eyes. "Thank you. It's been hard enough, saying goodbye to Mom, but I don't know how to help McKenna."

A sob shook her body, and Andrew came forward and took her in his arms, just as he'd done with her daughter. The helplessness in Sarah's eyes was familiar to him. He'd seen it in the eyes of everyone trying to help him when they'd realized their tactics didn't work.

"You're doing the best you can," Andrew whispered into Sarah's hair. "McKenna is lucky to have a mom who cares so much about her."

His words made him ashamed of how he'd been treating everyone in his life. They, too, had been doing the best they could, trying to help him the best way they knew how. And he'd shoved them all away.

"Thank you," Sarah said, pulling away and dabbing at her eyes. "I need to get in there. You'll be out here?"

He nodded. "Or in the community room. I'm here for a healthy living seminar, and they have some great snacks. Is it all right if McKenna and I go have a few? Does she have any food allergies?"

"That sounds fine, and no, no food allergies." Sarah turned her attention to her daughter. "You behave yourself, all right? Mind your manners, and I'll see you soon."

McKenna went over to her mother and gave her a hug. "I will. Thanks for letting me go with him."

Sarah turned and walked back to the sanctuary, and Andrew took McKenna's hand. "Are you hungry?"

As McKenna smiled at him and nodded, some of the heaviness in his chest seemed to disappear. He'd have a lot of amends to make, but it seemed easier to face the future knowing there was someone looking up to him.

**

Jealousy ripped through Layla as she watched Andrew hug the willowy blonde woman. She would never be willowy or blonde, and those facts had never bothered her until now. Didn't Andrew have rules about touching women?

Maybe Javier was right. Why was she attracted to a man who was so clearly off limits?

She took a deep breath and went back into the community room. She hadn't wanted to interrupt the breakout sessions that had already started, which was why she'd come down here. Bad decision.

At least she could turn it into a good decision by drinking some of the yummy fruit-infused water her cousin's restaurant had provided. Maybe some hydration would clear the murky thoughts in her brain.

Fortunately a few other people were milling around the community room, making it impossible for Layla to brood.

However, after she got her drink and turned to find a place to sit, she saw Andrew re-enter the room, holding a little girl's hand. She recognized the little girl as being with Andrew when he'd hugged the woman. Was it too much to hope that they were relatives or something? Andrew usually didn't associate with anyone, except to politely nod and make it look like he was somewhat civil.

He was coming straight towards her. "Hi Layla. This is my friend, McKenna. Her mom is letting her hang out with us for a while."

"My Nana died," the child said somberly. "Andrew understands how I feel."

Layla stared at him. She couldn't see him engaging in someone else's grief when he had such a poor handle on his own.

"And McKenna understands how I feel," Andrew said. "I'm glad we ran into you, because talking with McKenna and her mom made me realize that I've been hard on you. I know you're just trying to help, and I've been . . ."

He shook his head slowly, then looked down at the little girl before looking back at her. "Well, I've been a jerk. To you, to everyone really. We all handle grief differently, and my way is . . ."

Tears filled his eyes, and Layla watched as the little girl put her arm around him.

"It's okay, Andrew. I hafta say sorry to my mom too. I told her I hated her, and that's a lie. I was just mad because she was making me come here. But my mom is sad, too, isn't she?"

Whatever he'd been trying to tell Layla was seemingly forgotten as Andrew knelt and hugged the little girl. "She sure is. But we have to figure out how to stop making other people sad just because we are."

Layla couldn't help the tears in her own eyes as she watched

Andrew interact with the child. She grabbed a box of tissues from a nearby table and held it out to them.

"Here. Looks like you guys could use this."

Andrew smiled. "Thanks. I was trying to apologize, in case you didn't get all that."

"I did." Layla took a deep breath. "And I suppose I also owe you an apology. You're right that we all handle grief differently. It must be frustrating for you to hear everyone telling you how you're supposed to do it, and when you're supposed to get over your fiancée's death."

"It's the worst," McKenna said. "At least Andrew didn't make me go look at Nana's creepy dead body. I don't want to have nightmares."

Layla tried to hide a smile at McKenna's indignant response. Andrew caught her eye, and they locked gazes. He wanted to laugh, too, but Layla was impressed at how considerate he was being of McKenna's feelings.

"How about we call it even?" he said, ruffling McKenna's hair. "Like I told this squirt, we're all doing the best we can, but sometimes in the midst of our own pain, we forget that about others while expecting them to understand that about us. So thanks for putting up with all my garbage."

Wow. Layla took a deep breath. It was like someone had just hit Andrew over the head with a wisdom stick. Javier's warning sounded in her head. She knew he wouldn't be ready for a relationship anytime soon, but . . .

Once again, she lamented the fact that someone who seemed to be so willing to examine himself was so completely off limits.

As if he knew the direction of Layla's thoughts, Javier walked up to them.

"Andrew!"

"Hey Javier. Meet my new friend, McKenna Stone."

"Sarah's little girl?"

Andrew nodded. "She didn't want to go to her grandmother's viewing, so I told her she could keep me company."

Javier looked surprised, glancing over at Layla. Another warning?

"I didn't know you had reconnected."

Andrew shrugged. "We did, just now. I'd forgotten about all the people here that have been part of my life for so long. Do you know the first thing she remembered about me was that I accidentally set Allie's dolls on fire?"

Layla couldn't help smiling at Javier's grin. "There was that one we did on purpose. I added the lighter fluid."

"Yeah, but that doll was evil. It had the creepiest grin. And those eyes . . . I'm telling you, we kept that thing from killing us all in our beds."

McKenna gasped, and Andrew's eyes widened. "Uh, I'm sure it wasn't really evil. I was just scared of it, that's all. Not that you should set anything on fire that scares you. Javier and I got into a lot of trouble for that, and we had to volunteer at the fire department for a month to make up for it."

Javier chuckled. "And we had to buy Allie a new doll. Who'd have thought people spent a hundred dollars on a doll?"

"I don't like dolls," McKenna said. "I like tractors. Andrew is going to ask my mom if I can help him with his tractor. I might even get to ride in it."

The exchange was no big deal, except a little more of the man Andrew hid underneath his gruff exterior came out. The more he showed, the harder it was for Layla not to like him. True, a guy who set his sister's dolls on a fire didn't seem like the most upstanding of citizens, but there was an innocence in the reminiscence that made Layla smile.

"What trouble are you two up to now?"

Allie, Andrew's sister, approached, a suspicious look on her face. Layla hadn't spent much time talking with her, since she was always working, so it was nice to see her here.

Allie turned to Layla. "Do not let them spend much time together. Mayhem always ensues." Then she grinned. "Or at least be sure you get an invitation to the party. What havoc are we wreaking today?"

"None," Andrew said. "I'm helping out my friend McKenna here. You might remember her mom, Sarah, our old babysitter. Sarah very helpfully reminded me of your poor beloved dolls."

Allie laughed. "I still have a few with scorch marks as a reminder of what jerks boys can be."

Then Allie bent to McKenna. "If Andrew asks you if you want to be part of his space experiments, just say no."

McKenna's eyes widened. "Why? I like space stuff. I want to go to Mars someday. We read a magazine in school about missions to Mars."

"It's hopeless, then." Allie shook her head, a smile on her face as she looked at Andrew. "I see you've found a minion to carry out your plans."

Andrew shrugged. "Just a happy coincidence." Then he turned to McKenna. "But we do have a rocket-building project at the day camp. You're going to love it."

"Maybe I'll get another new doll out of the deal." Allie turned to Layla. "He ruined this super expensive, but super hideous doll our Aunt Camille sent, so Gram made him earn the money to buy me a new one. Only I got to pick the one I really wanted instead of the monstrosity from Aunt Camille."

Javier stared at her. "Wait a second. You didn't even like the doll we ruined?"

"No," Allie said, making a noise. "Her name was Creepella, because she was so creepy."

"See!" Andrew gestured wildly. "All this time, you and I have been carrying a bad reputation, and it wasn't entirely deserved."

Allie started laughing, and the men soon joined in. This must have been what Andrew had been like before Mykel died. And as Andrew bent to say something else to little McKenna, Layla couldn't help hoping that she'd see more of this man in the future.

Chapter Nine

Andrew felt a lightness in his heart that he hadn't felt in years. Certainly not since Mykel's death. Gram had invited Sarah over to the house after Nellie's funeral, and somehow that had involved Javier, Layla, and a few random people Andrew should probably know except didn't remember.

He'd definitely been in a fog since returning to Arcadia Valley. These people were friends, neighbors, and almost like family, and he'd shoved them all aside like they were nothing.

Caroline came to sit by him and handed him a glass of Gram's homemade tea. "I hear you accepted another camper."

"Sorry." He took a long sip. "McKenna seemed so lost, and I know what that feels like. I told her she could be my helper, so you don't have to worry about finding extra supplies or getting more help."

"Good. Because that college kid I hired no-showed today. When I finally got ahold of her, she gave me some lame excuse, then quit."

Andrew gave his cousin a sympathetic look. "I'm sorry. That really stinks. Are you going to need me to help out?"

"We should be fine. Mom's been giving me a hand, and she's oddly been enjoying it."

He followed Caroline's gaze across the room to where her mom sat with Gram and some of Gram's friends, talking as though there'd never been a rift.

"It's amazing how much she's changed over the past few months," Andrew said, returning his gaze to Caroline.

"Believe it or not, I have you to thank for that. We were making progress, but she and Gram were still having a lot of trouble. According to Mom, you said something to her that got her thinking. About not treating Gram like the enemy. And, she's reading her Bible again."

Though her words were meant as a compliment, they made him feel even more guilty about how he'd been treating Layla. He'd apologized, but it still felt like he hadn't done enough.

"It's easy enough to give the advice, but a lot harder to live it out yourself," he said, scanning the crowd for Layla.

"Looking for a certain nurse? I hear there have been some pretty impressive sparks."

He looked back at her. "Don't go there. I'd be lying if I said I wasn't attracted to her, but I just . . ." Andrew shook his head. "I can't. For as many times as I think, what if, with Layla, I miss Mykel a thousand more. It's not fair to Layla to pursue something when I know I can never give her my whole heart."

Caroline took his hand and squeezed. "I know it feels like you're still stuck, but that admission is progress. You used to not even say Mykel's name and would get mad if any of us did. You also would have never admitted to being attracted to anyone else."

He squeezed back, then pulled her into a side hug. "Thanks. Believe it or not, I didn't think it was possible to be attracted to anyone besides Mykel."

As if everyone knew what they were talking about, the crowd parted, and Layla was coming towards them.

"I know it's too soon for you to say something to her, but I hope you'll give Layla an honest chance. She's a nice person, and it isn't good for you to be alone."

Not being alone didn't seem like a strong enough reason to pursue a relationship. He knew a lot of people were in relationships, not because they genuinely cared for the other person, but because they couldn't stand the idea of being alone. It didn't seem fair to do that, and Layla definitely deserved better than that.

That was the problem. Every time he thought about pursuing Layla, he thought about how she deserved better than a guy who liked her but would probably never love her as much as she deserved.

"I hope I'm not interrupting," Layla said. "Enid wanted me to make sure you all got something to eat."

"We did, thanks," Caroline patted the empty chair next to her. "Why don't you join us?"

Layla's eyes sought his, as if asking for permission. Did she understand his struggle? How he wanted to do the right thing, but wasn't sure what that was?

"Please," he said, giving her an encouraging smile. "No state secrets being discussed here, just shop talk that I think we got squared away."

Smiling, Layla took the chair Caroline indicated. "Good. I'm trying not to butt in too much, but I hope that means you're all working on some of the stress management techniques I shared with you. Enid seems to be doing incredibly well, so keeping the family issues that plague her in check will sustain that progress."

Caroline gave a small laugh. "Whew. No wonder you two go rounds. Anyone who can tell Andrew what to do and live to tell the tale has to be made of strong stuff. But to answer your question, yes. Other than a small staffing hiccup, and Andrew's very generous offer to a grieving little girl, things with the day camp are finally on an even keel. Hayden is meeting with some investors later this week, and we've even seen Allie emerge from her cave. Life on Bigby Farm is about as good as it gets."

Caroline patted his leg. "And speaking of life being good, I see my fiancé has just returned from his errand, so I'm going to go spend some time with him. Think about what I said."

She gave him a wink then sauntered off, probably feeling a little too proud of herself that she'd managed to get Andrew and Layla alone.

"Do you agree with her assessment?" Layla turned her attention on him, and he wasn't sure if she was teasing, playing her nurse role, or if there was something else behind her question.

"I do. Gram and Aunt Camille are also getting along better, which is miraculous, if you ask me. I've never seen them enjoying each other's company so much."

Layla seemed to be studying his face. Sometimes he hated when she looked at him like that. It was almost as if she was trying to figure him out, and he wasn't sure if he wanted her to.

"What about the rest of your family? Are they still putting pressure on your grandmother?"

Chiding himself for being a fool, Andrew shook his head. As Allie used to tell him all the time, everything was not about him. Sometimes he forgot that Layla's true purpose in being there was to take care of his grandmother, not to worry about him.

"Not lately. I think they're all hopeful that Hayden's plan to turn the farm into a destination resort will bring in some decent income, and then they'll try for a share of that. But we'll see. With my family, you never know."

Layla nodded, and even though she didn't have a pen and paper in her hand, Andrew could see she was making notes.

"What about your parents? You haven't mentioned them."

Ah, the great question Andrew had hoped not to answer. Funny that he'd rather talk about Mykel than them.

"My father is the current ringleader of the gang trying to put Gram in a home. I'm sure his motivation is partially about getting her money and getting her out of the way, but he's also upset that Allie and I have, to use his words, buried ourselves here."

The expression on Layla's face made him wish he hadn't used the word, buried. She had used that on him as well, and while she meant it in the sense of his loss, his parents didn't see it that way.

"He's not worried about my grief," Andrew added quickly. "He just hates that we're here and not in Seattle. He likes the city life and resents the fact that both Allie and I have chosen to remain on the farm. Dad spent a lot of years working towards his goal of living in the city. When I lived there briefly, I think he thought that I'd come to see things his way."

The conversation he'd just had with Caroline replayed in his head, as did the words he'd used with Layla initially about seeing things from the patient's perspective, and not forcing her agenda on them.

Did he know what his father thought? Why his father was acting like this? They'd all assumed it was greed, but could his father have other motivations?

"Is everything okay?" Layla asked, concern filling her face. "I lost you there for a minute."

"Just thinking about things. It's been a while since I've actually talked to my father instead of fought with him. You've reminded me that we can disagree but still find common ground."

As much as he wasn't sure he wanted to admit it, having Layla in his life had brought about a lot of positive changes. She made him think in deeper ways, making him want to . . . be a better man.

The realization startled him.

Mykel had challenged him in similar ways, loving him, yet also pushing him to do things that were hard but beneficial. When she died, he'd stopped trying to improve, not caring about the kind of man he was.

And now...

Andrew looked across the crowd to where Hayden had his arm around Caroline, and his cousin looked like she had never been happier. Then Allie's laugh rang out, and Andrew realized just how much he'd been neglecting his sister.

One more case of where he'd been assuming, not looking at things from her perspective. Was working at the Gas N' Shop what she really wanted? Was there another way?

McKenna was talking to another little girl, and Andrew thought about how he didn't want that sweet child to fall into the pit where he'd been living. Layla had been right that he was wasting his life in the grave when he was still alive. Mykel would be ashamed of the way he'd hidden himself. And, he was pretty sure Nellie wouldn't want McKenna to spend the next few years of her life brooding.

Layla had asked him what his dream for himself was. Andrew wasn't entirely sure, but there was a spark inside him, coming to life, and telling him it was time to live again.

"I'm sorry," Layla said, interrupting his thoughts. "I should leave you alone. You've clearly got other things on your mind."

As she stood to leave, he thought about sharing those thoughts with her and asking her to stay. But they were just glimmers right then, and he wasn't sure he could act on them. Plus, he wasn't sure he wanted to give her hope.

Not when he barely dared hope himself.

**

Layla hated walking away, but clearly Andrew didn't want her company. Who could blame him? Why did she have this compulsion to keep asking him difficult questions? Why couldn't she ask him something normal, something simple, like, "What are your hobbies?"

No, she'd had to ask him about his parents, because she knew there was some level of estrangement, and he'd clearly never mentioned them. For a reason.

Javier and Molly stood by the food table, laden with leftovers from the health seminar at the church.

"Look at all this food!" Layla tried to sound cheerful, since she didn't want another lecture from Javier about not pinning her hopes on Andrew. She'd gotten that message loud and clear.

"You just can't leave him alone, can you?" Javier said, grinning.

Molly elbowed him in the ribs. "Would you stop? They need to figure things out for themselves. From the way Andrew can't take his eyes off her, there's obviously something there. But you know what he's like when pushed."

Layla looked over to the spot she'd vacated, feeling the weight of Andrew's observation. But just as quickly as she turned her head, he'd averted his gaze.

Why did he have to be so difficult? It was like she'd told him that first day in her apartment. She wasn't looking for a marriage proposal, but the more she got to know him, the more she couldn't help thinking there might be something between them worth pursuing. At least exploring.

Caroline approached, and she looked slightly annoyed. Or at least it was a similar expression to Andrew's annoyed look. You'd almost think they were brother and sister instead of cousins.

"Why did you leave Andrew all alone?"

Layla shrugged. "He didn't seem to be very interested in conversation. Rather, he was lost in his own thoughts. I felt like I was a bother." Then, remembering how she'd already been chastising herself, she added, "I also think I got too personal with my questions. I don't know why I can't keep the conversation limited to safe topics, like the weather, how the tractor is running, or something like that."

Caroline laughed. "Good luck with that. None of us are into

that sort of thing. If we wanted to have a conversation like that, we'd go visit one of the grannies. Or, worse, give one of the aunts or uncles a call."

Yet another mysterious reference to the dysfunctional Bigby family. Except Caroline treated it like it was almost a joke, rather than something painful the way Andrew did. The way Enid did.

"I know it sounds like I'm prying, but I would love to hear more about your family. Even though Enid is doing great, I still worry about her. Though bringing up her children makes her angry, I also sense a deep sadness. Like she misses them but won't admit it. Managing stress is an important element of keeping your grandmother healthy. I know this isn't the right time, but it would mean a lot if we could sit down and talk about it sometime."

Caroline didn't answer, but glanced over at where Andrew sat. He hadn't moved. Then she turned her attention back to Layla. "The trouble with what's wrong with our family is that I don't think it's as simple as just a disagreement. I think Gram has a different problem with each of her children. In the case of my mother, there was definitely a lot of misunderstanding. They're working through it."

Layla's heart warmed as she watched Caroline look around until her gaze landed on her mother and softened. "We're working on it. But for things to work out with Gram and her other children, I'm not sure I can help you."

Shaking her head, Caroline gave Layla an apologetic look. "My grandmother is a stubborn woman, and even though I'm sure she's probably also partially at fault in all of the situations, she's not willing to make the first move. It's going to take a lot of apologies from everyone else before she softens. And, if you haven't guessed it with your interactions with Andrew, we're a pretty stubborn bunch."

Then Caroline turned to Javier and grinned. "I'm not joking about our stubbornness, am I?"

Javier and Molly laughed. Then Javier said, "I'm fairly certain that the word stubborn didn't exist in the dictionary until you all came along."

Then he gave Molly a smile that warmed Layla's heart. She hoped someday that a man would look at her that same way.

"I learned from the best of them," Javier said. "And then I refined stubbornness to a point that made me almost unbearable. Fortunately, I learned from my mistakes."

He turned his attention back to Layla. "But maybe stubbornness is a Quintana trait as well. As much as you've been warned off about Andrew, you can't seem to give up."

Layla didn't answer as her gaze wandered back to Andrew. McKenna had brought one of her friends over to him and was showing him something. She couldn't see what it was, but she saw the light on Andrew's face.

Why would she like someone so stubborn? He pushed her away at every turn, and his irrational attachment to his grief prevented him from living a full life.

Because deep down, Andrew couldn't hide the caring spirit that lurked within. She dealt with patients who were difficult, patients whose families were difficult, but none of them had the depth of love that Andrew did. Most of the difficulties she'd had with patients were that they were too lazy to do the work, didn't want to deal with the expense, or simply didn't care enough to listen to reason.

DANICA FAVORITE

When she'd passed his truck earlier, she'd noticed that the articles she'd printed out for him with information about diabetes were sitting on the front seat, highlighted. Obviously by him. Maybe he did fight her, but he wasn't fighting for fighting's sake. He truly wanted the best for his grandmother.

How could she hate him for that?

She could understand his grief, knowing how deeply he cared for others. She could even understand the fact that he didn't want to get involved with anyone else. If he felt that deeply about others, it must be a scary proposition to face falling in love and risking losing someone.

"You've got it bad, don't you?" Caroline teased, bringing Layla's attention back to her friends' amused expressions.

"What am I supposed to do? It would be easy to let go and give up, but I feel like I'm selling him short. But I also don't want to go chasing where I'm not wanted."

"I wish I knew the answer," Caroline said. "We've all tried to help him in our own way, but until he's ready, there isn't anything any of us can do."

Whatever the girls had been talking to Andrew about, they wrapped up their discussion then went running past where Layla stood, laughing and jabbering amongst themselves. Andrew looked pleased. Like he knew he'd brought a ray of sunshine into a couple of children's lives.

"He's so good with children," Layla said, trying not to let that be one more thing she liked about him.

The trouble was, the more she tried not to like Andrew, to push him out of her mind, the more he seemed impossible to resist.

Clearly there was something wrong with her.

Why did she have such a pathological need to chase men who didn't want her?

A tiny voice inside her argued that Andrew needed her.

But was that good enough? How many women stayed in bad relationships because of that excuse? She'd obviously stayed with Troy for that dumb reason.

As much as she kept saying Andrew needed therapy, maybe she was the one who needed a counselor.

Another car pulled into the driveway, and Layla shook her head. Moping about the situation in the middle of a party wasn't healthy, either.

It was amazing how quickly word had traveled about what she'd assumed was a small get together. At the church, Enid had told them that a few people were coming to the house. Javier had offered to bring leftovers from the health seminar. Layla couldn't imagine what would've happened had he not done so. Knowing Enid, she probably would have found a way to prepare a bunch of refreshments herself. Maybe that was why Andrew was so irresistible to her. She knew that he came from the sort of place that she'd always wished she'd come from.

"Oh boy," Caroline said. She turned to Layla. "Well, if you were curious about the family dynamic, you're about to get a load of it for yourself. Andrew's dad just showed up."

"I thought Andrew said he lived in Seattle."

"He does," Caroline said. "And I'm pretty sure that this isn't going to be a happy reunion."

Layla looked over at Andrew to see if he had noticed. He'd already gotten up and was starting for the car.

She glanced back at Caroline, who said, "I need to find Allie. Javier, go back up Andrew, because even though he'll tell us all that he's fine, he's going to need some support. The last time Uncle Bart was here, it turned into a shouting match."

If Caroline was concerned about a shouting match starting, she didn't have to wait long. Before his cousin was even out of earshot, Layla could hear Andrew's voice. Not the words, but enough of the tone to confirm the tension in the family.

Even though no one had given her the job, and it had been Javier who'd been specifically asked to go help, she found herself headed in Andrew's direction.

When Layla arrived, Bart was shouting something about stock his son had no right to sell.

"I have every right," Andrew said. "It's mine to do with as I choose. And I chose to sell it."

"I didn't spend all those years working so you could throw it away," Bart said.

Layla tried not to cringe. Based on Enid's complaints about her children, the fights always centered around money. And here was Andrew, fighting with his father over it. Why did families let dollars separate blood?

"I don't see it as throwing it away. I'm investing in my sister and her dreams."

Bart appeared to calm down. "Has she decided to finish college then?"

Andrew shook his head. "College isn't the right path for everyone," he said. "Allie isn't good at school, nor does she want to go. We've been through this. If you're not going to support your daughter's dreams, then I will."

Layla's heart broke a little for Allie, knowing how hard it was to have a father who didn't support your passion. She hated how she wasn't getting along with her own father because of her love for Mexican culture. But the fact that Andrew was doing something to stand up for Allie warmed Layla's heart.

"She needs to grow up and get some responsibility, not work in a gas station. What kind of career path is that? There's no future for her."

Andrew finally seemed to realize that Layla had approached. Javier was standing back, as if he was waiting to see what would happen before getting involved.

Andrew looked at her. "Well," he said. "You wanted to know about my family, so here you go. I inherited some stocks from my grandparents on my mother's side. Allie needed some new processing equipment for her lavender, so I sold the stock to buy it. Being a good brother makes me a bad son. Especially since Dad keeps hoping Allie's business will fail so she has to go back and finish the education that he spent so much money on."

With a sigh, Andrew turned back to his father. "I know you love Allie, and you want what's best for her. She's a grown woman, so you need to talk to her and find out what she wants."

Caroline returned, looking frustrated. "Hi Uncle Bart," she said, sounding breathless.

"This doesn't concern you," Bart said. "I want to talk to my son. Alone."

Andrew made an exasperated noise. It was nice to know that for once it wasn't directed at her. However, that probably wasn't a very good thought considering it meant that there was clearly a lot of trouble about to go down.

"I've said all I've got to say. My Grandma Russell left me that money, and there were no restrictions on how I was to spend it. Those stocks weren't doing me any good, and Allie needs the money to expand her lavender business."

Bart's face reddened. "Why are you encouraging her in this foolishness?"

"She has an excellent business plan. That's not foolishness, but a sign of a talented woman who's done a lot of thinking and planning to make her dreams come true. If I can invest in that, I will."

Could a man make himself any more endearing? None of Andrew's fights were about himself, but about helping someone else.

But that wasn't a good enough answer for Bart. "And how much of your resources have you thrown at this? I know this isn't the first time you've given your sister money, and it probably won't be the last. When is enough, enough?"

The man's face had turned red, and Layla could see the spittle flying from his lips.

"It's none of your business. It's my money, I'll spend it how I want to."

Layla recognized the frustration in Andrew's voice from the set of his jaw and the way his brow furrowed. His father wore the same expression. She was starting to recognize it as the stubborn Bigby look. Basically, no one was going to win this argument.

Then Andrew's expression changed. He looked at his father, and said slowly, "What is this really about? You say you want the best for us, but you're not willing to listen to what we want. I know it's scary to watch your children struggle. But Dad, I'm tired of fighting. I'm sorry you don't like the decisions I've made. But I'm doing my best to do the right thing. So how about we find a way to figure things out together?"

Andrew's words gave Layla hope for the situation. Andrew was doing exactly what they had talked about with Enid's care. He was trying to find common ground with his father rather than fighting. Though it seemed like a subtle change, it was enough to make Layla think that other changes could happen in Andrew's heart as well.

Unfortunately, Bart looked at Andrew like he'd said something absolutely moronic. Andrew shifted his weight, but he didn't say anything. Caroline went over to Andrew and put her arm around him. Solidarity between cousins fighting similar battles with their parents-to be recognized and understood by them.

Wasn't that the battle they all faced? Wanting to be seen as the human beings they'd become, not what their parents wanted them to be? Even Layla knew that fight. To be an American who embraced her Mexican roots, not the picture-perfect American ideal her father wanted for her.

While Andrew had to face his grief alone, this was one place where Layla could stand beside him and offer her friendship and support.

Maybe it would turn into letting her into other areas as well.

Chapter Ten

The anger hadn't left his father's face, Andrew realized with a sinking feeling. Even though he was trying to be reasonable and see things from his perspective, or at least find a way to compromise, his words only seemed to make the other man angrier.

"We have a legacy to protect, and I don't think you're taking it very seriously," his father said, using the same tone he'd used when Andrew brought home grades that weren't up to par. After all, an A minus should have been an A.

But this wasn't about Andrew's childhood. This was about how Andrew had spent the past few years doing everything he could to save the farm.

"Taking it seriously? That's ridiculous. What do you think I'm fighting for?"

Andrew looked around the property, remembering how run-down things had become during his years in Seattle. Sure, he'd come on vacations and done what he could, and Allie and Caroline had done quite a bit. But they'd lacked the money for the big improvements, and their time was spent just keeping things going, not on major overhauls. When Andrew sold everything he owned and moved here, he'd provided a much-needed infusion of cash into the operation. It hadn't been enough, but it had been a start.

"I've been killing myself here, trying to save it. Doesn't that count for something?"

Caroline rubbed his back gently, giving him support. She hadn't wanted to accept his money, but once she realized that he was in it just as much as she was, they'd become a team.

"The family farm is dying," his father said. "You need to get with the future and not waste time on something that will inevitably end."

"Everything will end at some point," Andrew said. "Nothing lasts forever, except God, and the things God makes. But it doesn't mean we don't fight for the things we think are worth fighting for. The things worth living for. Maybe that doesn't mean anything to you, but the farm is everything to me."

Then Andrew took a deep breath and shifted his weight, stepping away from his cousin's support. Andrew had to do this on his own. He'd never told anyone what he was about to say, but maybe it would make a difference. He glanced over at Layla, who'd been giving him encouraging looks. She'd asked him to come to terms with his grief, and he'd fought her on it. In his counseling session, he'd only given enough information to get everyone off his back. But maybe it was time to let it out.

He squared his shoulders and stared right at his father. "When Mykel died, I lost my purpose in life. I wasn't suicidal, at least not in the sense where I contemplated doing harm to myself. But every day I wondered why I bothered getting out of bed in the morning. Saving the farm gave me something to live for. Allie's crazy dream was the only reason I was able to put one foot in front of the other. Maybe that's not good enough for you, but it was the only thing that gave me the will to live."

Then Andrew turned to Layla. She was part of this too. "You told me I buried myself with Mykel, and you were partially right. But as I look at Gram, Caroline, and Allie, I did have a reason to live. Supporting them, taking care of them, and helping them pursue their dreams. I just didn't realize it until now."

He sighed. Suddenly he felt more exhausted than he had in a long time. "I haven't allowed myself to want anything for myself since Mykel died."

Andrew took a step toward Layla, feeling shaky and weak. But with the pushing she'd done, she had to understand. Had to know. "Before Mykel got sick, I considered myself the luckiest man alive. I had a great job, a gorgeous condo, a fancy car, a woman who made me happier than I could have imagined, and a family that I thought stood by me."

He glanced over at his father, who at least wore the expression of a man who was thinking about his words. Hopefully he would finally understand where Andrew was coming from.

"When she died, I realized something. None of that means anything. None of those things saved the woman I loved. And none of those things cared about me."

Shaking his head slowly, he took a deep breath before looking his father in the eye. "I lied to you. I didn't quit my job. They fired me, because after she died, I couldn't bring myself to leave my bed. I was a zombie, and I refused to do anything. Allie came to see me with one of her weird concoctions, and she told it me was okay. She sat with me, in my dirty, stinky condo, and held me while I cried."

Tears filled his eyes as he remembered his sister's kindness. He knew Caroline had gone looking for her, but hadn't found her. Knowing Allie, she was up in the hayloft, cuddling some kittens until Andrew told her it was safe to come out. Their father might think Allie was a screw-up, but she'd probably saved Andrew's life.

"Allie is the only person who let me be who I needed to be in the midst of my pain. She's never tried to fix me, she's just loved me. I support her unconditionally because that's how she supported me. It's how family should be."

His father looked wounded, but still ready to lash out. Everyone had done so much hurting each other that it no longer felt like a victory to score points.

Maybe it wasn't a direct lesson he'd learned from Layla, but because of his interactions with her, he knew there was a better way. His father was only the enemy because he'd made him so.

Andrew gave a small nod to Layla, then held out his hand to Caroline. His cousin had humbled herself to take the first step with her parents, and even though Andrew still wasn't sure of his relationship with Aunt Camille, Caroline had shown him that amends could be made.

Fortunately, Caroline seemed to understand what was going on, and she came back to his side and put her arm around him. Surprisingly, Layla did the same, coming around his other side, and her touch was more of a comfort than he would have thought.

"Dad, I know it feels like an insult to you that I've changed my life so drastically. I can see where it would be upsetting to you to have worked all those years to put both me and Allie through college, only to feel like we've just thrown it in your face. I appreciate everything you've done for us. More than I have said, and I probably should have done so."

He couldn't read his father's expression, but even if it only made him angrier, Andrew had to try to do the right thing.

"Living in Seattle with Mykel, having dinner with you and Mom once a week, that life was like a dream. Some days, I miss it. And even though I enjoyed my job, I get more satisfaction out of a newly cleared field, fixing a piece of equipment for Gram, or smelling the fresh-cut lavender. I got everything I ever dreamed of. It seems only right to help others do the same."

Andrew looked around at the farm. The barn with the new roof he'd put on, the fields he'd helped plow for Allie's lavender crop, the children's area he and Caroline had built, and even the repairs to Gram's house. He'd done good here. And though he'd never allowed himself to express or feel that emotion since Mykel's death, he'd have to admit, he was happy.

He had a good life. Maybe not the same life he'd had with Mykel, and maybe it wasn't what he'd pictured, but suddenly, he was overwhelmed with gratitude that God had allowed him to live in such a wonderful way.

Andrew wiggled out of the embraces of the women supporting him and stepped forward to his father. He held out a hand, hoping his father would take it.

"I'm sorry, Dad. I hope you'll forgive me for all the things I've done to not live up to the man you want me to be. It would mean a lot if you'd take the time to get to know the man I am instead."

His father looked at Andrew's outstretched hand. For a moment, Andrew wasn't sure he would take it. But then, his father pulled him into a hug.

It was a bear of a hug, the kind Andrew remembered from his childhood.

"I'm sorry, too, Son." As quickly as the hug began, his father stepped away, then looked him up and down. "I didn't realize Mykel's death had been so hard on you. We all thought you'd moved on."

Andrew wanted to argue and say that if his father had actually spent time with him and gotten to know him now, he'd know that. It seemed obvious to everyone else in town.

He glanced over his shoulder at Layla. Until now, he'd never imagined himself saying the words, but as he'd rehearsed them in his head, it seemed time to let them roll off his tongue.

"I refused to move on. But I think it's time I started figuring it out."

**

The words stunned Layla, but Caroline gave her a squeeze as though they were to be expected.

"But we still have to talk about those stocks," Bart said. "You can't just throw the money away like that on your sister's foolish plans."

Caroline stilled beside Layla, and a dark expression filled Andrew's face. He stood there, silent for a moment, like he was considering his words before speaking. Though father and son seemed to have reached a new understanding, the family still had a long way to go.

"With all due respect," Andrew said. "I will not discuss my finances with you. I'm not sure how you found out about the stocks, but it's none of your business."

Bart looked like he was about to launch into another tirade, but Andrew shook his head. "Don't. This can't be about money. Money is the least important thing to me. But if that's what stands in the way of our relationship, I'll go cash out what's left of my 401K and give it all to you."

The older man looked shocked. Even Layla couldn't fathom such an offer, except that in all her conversations with Andrew, she'd gotten the sense that money truly wasn't important to him. Hadn't that been one of the first things he'd warned her about in not being a great catch?

"That's not necessary," Bart said, shifting nervously. "You worked hard for what's in your 401K, that's your money."

At least Bart could show signs of being reasonable. Though Andrew said money wasn't important to him, he looked relived that his father wasn't taking him up on his offer.

Andrew nodded slowly, then looked in the direction of the barn. "As for your thoughts on Allie, you need to give her a chance. Sure, she does things her own way, and she's never taken the traditional route. But she's a good person. And, to be honest, one of the smartest people I've ever met. Anytime you want to talk, we can talk. But I will not tolerate anyone badmouthing Allie."

Such loyalty seemed almost impossible to argue with. And, it served to reinforce Layla's growing feelings for him. Was there any hope, considering he'd just told his father he was ready to move on?

For a moment, Bart looked like he was going to argue, but

Andrew gave him a firm look. "I think we've said enough for one day. You should go say hi to Aunt Camille, and then you two can both give your regards to Gram."

Concern rose in Layla at Andrew's mention of his grandmother, but Caroline whispered, "It's okay, he'll be fine if Mom is with him. That's why Andrew suggested he see her first."

"I didn't know Camille was here," Bart said, looking around.

"I'm sure she'd love to see you." Andrew gave a small smile, then an absolutely exhausted expression filled his face.

Layla went over to him and linked arms with him. "Weren't you going to show me the new, um, place, where Allie is planting her lavender?"

She had no idea what she was talking about, but surely the mention of Allie and lavender would keep Bart from following.

Andrew blinked, shook his head slowly as if to clear the cobwebs out, then nodded. "That's right. I forgot. Dad, if you'll excuse us."

Bart didn't seem to notice, or think it was rude for the abrupt exit. Then again, he was already walking in the direction they'd pointed for Camille.

If that was what family warmth was like, then maybe Layla hadn't been missing out. But as she spied Javier and Molly cuddled on one of the benches and laughing, she knew that some families, like the one she'd come to Arcadia Valley to get to know, weren't so terrible.

Andrew led Layla to the other side of the barn, away from the people, but with a view of the lavender fields. They hadn't yet started blooming, but the area was still fragrant, with the buds ready to burst out in glorious display at any time.

"I can't believe I've been coming here all this time, and I haven't yet seen this," Layla said, inhaling the scent.

"I'm pretty sure this is your first social call." Andrew went to sit on one of the straw bales stacked along the back of the barn. "You haven't had much time to get the full tour."

Layla turned to him and smiled. "I'm glad I finally got the chance. I hope it was okay that I took you away, but you seemed like you were ready to get out of there."

He nodded. "I'm not good at talking about all that stuff. It had to be said, but . . ."

Shaking his head, Andrew stopped, then focused his attention on the fields before them. The green and purple were magnificent, even without it being peak season.

For a moment, it was enough to be out there with Andrew, observing the scenery. But Layla longed for more. A connection. She went and sat next to him.

"You were very brave. Most people wouldn't have said all that. Thank you for allowing me to be a part of it."

He looked sideways at her. "Did I have a choice? You're the one who's been pushing me all this time."

"It was for your own good." She smiled at him, then gently nudged him with her elbow. "And I have to say, I'm really impressed by how much you've changed. I know it's been hard, but I think it will be worth it in the end."

"You think?" Andrew chuckled, then nudged her back. "I'm sure you're probably right, but don't be getting a big head about it or anything. Lately I've come to realize just how blessed I am. It seems like an insult to God to continue moping over what I've lost when I still have so much."

Layla smiled. "It's a good thing God forgives a multitude of sins, isn't it?"

"I do have a lot to be forgiven for."

His tone was light, and Layla examined his face for signs that it wasn't a joke, but then he pulled a piece of straw out of the hay bale and tossed it at her.

"Since you have no comment, I'll just have to add to the list of my sins. Surely you'll have something to say about my picking on an innocent woman."

He laughed, and it was one of the sweetest sounds she'd heard in a long time. Andrew was letting his guard down near her, and it felt good to be so trusted.

"I'm sure I've done my share of wrong," Layla said, smiling back at him. "But we seem to both be doing a good job of getting over it and forgiving one another, so in the grand scheme of things, we're doing just fine."

The return glance he gave her was all warmth, making her tingle all the way down to her toes.

Did he know the effect he had on her?

Was there even a remote chance for them?

Andrew patted her leg. "Thanks. It's good of you to keep putting up with me."

She turned her body towards him, giving him another smile. "Isn't that what friends are for?"

When he opened his mouth to speak, Layla shook her head. "You need to change your rules. Maybe that's a lot of change for you all at once, but not every woman on the planet is clamoring to marry you. It's time you move out of the Dark Ages and let yourself be open to the possibilities."

He glanced over at her, a look in his eyes she didn't recognize. "Maybe I'm not sure I want you as a friend."

Seriously? After everything? Layla started to move off the bale, but Andrew grabbed her hand.

"I want . . ." The longing in his eyes took away any need for words.

Layla leaned forward and kissed him. Briefly. Gently.

A spark shot through her unlike anything she'd ever known with such a brief contact. But as she came closer to deepen the kiss, Andrew pulled away.

"I can't," he said. "I'm sorry. I didn't mean to lead you on. I. . ."

Once again, she'd pushed too hard, too soon. Kissing him had been so stupid. He'd given a tiny opening, and she'd come through with a tank.

"It's fine," Layla said, shaking her head. "I shouldn't have. . ."

Andrew gave a tiny smile. "That's why I have my rules. Mykel was the only person I've ever kissed. I feel. . ."

He looked disgusted with himself. "Look, I'm not good at this. I'm not one of those guys who knows what to do when it comes to women. Mykel just sort of happened. And you. . ."

The look he gave her nearly broke her heart.

"I don't know what I'm doing, and part of me feels like I'm doing something wrong, like I'm cheating on Mykel. Which is crazy, because she's dead. But I can't shake the way I'm torn. It's not fair to you, or to me, to pursue anything."

He hopped off the bale, looking regretful as he shook his head. "I'm sorry. I can't do this."

All right then. How much more could she put herself out

there for a guy who'd done everything he could to put on the brakes? He might think he was interested, and maybe he was, just a little. But clearly Layla was far more invested in finding out what was between them.

Maybe she had spent too much of her life chasing men who didn't want her. Her dad, Troy, and even Andrew.

But not anymore.

This time when Andrew walked away she let him.

Chapter Eleven

With mixed emotions, Layla pulled up to the Bigby farmhouse. On the seat next to her was a report from Enid's follow-up with the orthopedic surgeon. Everything had healed nicely, and thanks to Layla keeping her on track with her therapy, she was being released from care.

Happy news.

But as she saw Andrew showing McKenna something on the tractor, she couldn't help feeling a little disappointed that she wouldn't be spending as much time around him anymore. Though she'd let him walk away over a week before at the barn, part of her hoped he'd come chasing after her, telling her he'd been wrong to let her go.

But, like she'd already learned from the other men in her life, that never happened.

Even now, she couldn't help staring at her phone and wondering if her father was going to remember her birthday was today and give her a call. Which was completely stupid, considering he'd told her that if she pursued her foolish plans to get to know her mother's family, and as he put it, "turn

Mexican," he wasn't going to have anything to do with her. He'd told her to call when she stopped being ridiculous.

She hadn't heard from him since.

Maybe someday she'd learn.

As Layla got out of the car, McKenna hopped off the tractor and ran towards her.

"Guess what? Andrew says the tractor is almost fixed, and we can go for a ride on it soon."

Wiping his hands on a rag, Andrew joined them. "Hopefully this works. There aren't too many parts left to replace. I could have bought a new tractor for all the repairs I've done on this thing."

Layla smiled at him. "Why didn't you?"

The return smile was all warmth, and Layla couldn't help the flutter in her stomach. She tried to remind herself that it didn't mean anything, but it was hard to ignore how he looked at her. Like she meant something to him. Which was ridiculous, since in the two times since she'd seen him after the barn debacle, he'd been polite but gave no indication she was anything but his grandmother's caregiver.

"It was an exaggeration," Andrew said. "New tractors are more than we can afford, and at least with this old girl, I know all the parts and how they work. But this one has definitely proved to be a challenge. They don't make tractors like this anymore, and it's getting harder to find someone else to bounce ideas off."

Javier came around the other side of the house, along with a man Layla didn't recognize. Both were carrying large baskets of vegetables.

"Will that help you guys?" Andrew asked.

Javier set the basket he'd been carrying on the ground. "Ben said he can use all the vegetables at Corinna's Cupboard, and Abuela can dry the extra herbs. Are you sure you want us to take it all?"

Andrew shrugged. "It's more than we can use, and our booth at the Farmer's Market is smaller this year. We don't have the staffing capability, and Allie wants to focus on her lavender products. There are too many people selling vegetables for it to be cost effective for us to rent the additional space and hire someone to help."

Andrew turned to include Layla. "Do you know Ben Kujak? He runs Corinna's Cupboard, a local soup kitchen he manages in honor of his late wife. I've been talking to him about ways we can help men grieve in a society that doesn't always recognize the way men deal with losing a loved one."

He sure didn't waste any time, Layla would give him credit for that. It had only been two weeks since his breakthrough with McKenna, and now he was talking to other men about his loss?

Ben set his basket down and stepped forward to shake hands with Layla. "Nice to meet you. I presume you're Layla, Javier's cousin."

"Yes. Nice to meet you as well." She felt a twinge of disappointment that Ben knew of her in connection to Javier, not Andrew. But that was to be expected. It wasn't like they had any sort of relationship. Not even friendship.

"I can't tell you how glad I am that Andrew stopped by Grace Fellowship with flyers for his grief-support group. I've done a lot of healing after my wife's death, but I wish someone had come up with an idea like that when she first died. A lot of men are going to benefit from having a safe place to talk about their losses."

Andrew looked pleased with himself. "And, you got some food for the soup kitchen, so even better."

The men all seemed happy about the development, and even though McKenna probably had no idea what they were talking about, her grin matched Andrew's. But it rankled that Layla had been completely excluded from this latest move. True, he'd made it clear she didn't have a role in his life, but surely, with everything they'd talked about, he'd at least have told her he was starting a support group for grieving men.

"Can I help put the vegetables in Ben's truck?" McKenna asked. "I drew a picture for Maisie. Ben is going out with her mom."

Andrew ruffled McKenna's hair. "Sure thing, squirt. But come right back. I'm going to help Layla bring her things inside."

He walked over to her car as he always did, but Layla hung back. "I don't have anything to bring in today. Just stuff to take home."

"What? No Medieval torture devices?" He grinned, but it only served as a reminder that this would be Layla's last visit to the farm.

And even though she should be happy that he was treating her like a normal human being instead of acting scared of her like he had through most of Enid's treatment, she felt sick, knowing she was the only person struggling here.

But since it was only professional between them, she'd act professional.

"I'm sure you know her orthopedic visit went great. They don't think she needs additional therapy. She's also been doing well keeping up on her diabetes management."

Andrew studied her face. "But you disagree."

"No." Layla shook her head. "She hasn't needed her cane for a while now, and her diabetes numbers have been great. Your grandmother is fine, and I'm sure if she has her way, she's going to be talking Abuela into joining the Grannies for belly dancing lessons."

"Belly dancing?" Andrew gave her a strange look, and Layla smiled.

"Mona is having a One Thousand and One Arabian Nights themed party for her birthday this year, and she's decided that the Grannies are going to be the entertainment. She's trying to find a place that will rent out elephants for elephant rides as part of the festivities."

Andrew shook his head. "I'm assuming she's going to want to have the party here."

Layla shrugged. "You know them better than I do."

They stood in silence for a moment, staring at each other, then Andrew cleared his throat. "Well, I guess I should be letting you get to work. Let me know when you need me to help carry things out to your car."

Was he as hesitant to leave her company as she was his? "Andrew . . ." Layla took a deep breath. She had so many things she wanted to say to him, but she had no idea where to start.

He shifted his weight, like he wasn't sure he wanted to have this conversation with her, even though he had no idea what she was going to say. How could he, when she didn't even know?

"I just wanted to say that I've appreciated working with you to help your grandmother. We haven't always agreed, but you've challenged me in ways that have made me a better nurse. I'm really proud of you for all the work you've done in examining your grief and learning to move forward."

It sounded like a final goodbye. Even though she hoped it wouldn't be. But they didn't really have a reason to meet again, not unless he made an effort.

And she wasn't going to make the effort if he wasn't going to make the first step.

"I appreciate that," he said. "I'm glad we're parting as friends."

She tried to decipher his expression, but she hadn't fully learned how to read him yet.

"Are we friends?" she finally asked.

Andrew shrugged. "As much as we can be, I suppose."

"And your rules about being friends with females?"

Maybe she was being too forward, but she didn't want to play games. Nor did she want to cling to the hope of anything ever happening between them if he was going to be stubborn.

He made an annoyed sound. "Please don't push. I've been twisted and bent in so many new directions that I can't think about any other changes. That rule still stands. If we see each other on the street, we can be cordial, but I'm not ready for anything else."

"And what if something else finds you?"

Andrew closed his eyes. "I can't do this, Layla."

She took another deep breath. In the past, she'd never asked direct questions, never pushed for answers because she was afraid of what she'd find. But at least, if she asked, she'd know. Even if it meant she was mistaken in her feelings.

"Will you at least just answer this? Do you feel it? That there might be something between us?"

He shook his head slowly as he turned away. "I told you I'm not ready."

"You're right. I'm sorry. You've already made yourself clear."

She'd been wrong to keep pushing, because the expression on his face made it seem like he was well and truly done with her. Why couldn't she learn?

As Layla started for the door, Enid walked out, carrying a package. "Layla! I heard the good news!"

The old woman strode towards her like she was about to enter a speed walking contest.

Layla couldn't help smiling. She turned to glance in Andrew's direction, but he was already gone.

Let that be a lesson to her in hope.

"Don't mind him," Enid said. "He's been crabby ever since my good-for-nothing son dropped by to berate him. Camille tried to smooth things over when Bart came to say hi to me, but I saw how Andrew looked leaving the barn. You can't talk to him about anything, so I don't know what Bart said to upset him this time, but he's been in a fog ever since. The only thing that's cheered him is the time he's been spending over at the church, and talking about his plans for a men's grief group."

Layla's throat tightened. It wasn't Bart's words that had upset Andrew, but the fact that she'd kissed him. Part of her wanted to defend Bart and to say that they'd ended things on a positive note. But she wasn't sure she should admit that she'd thrown herself at Enid's grandson, either.

"You might have misinterpreted what happened," Layla said instead. "I'm sure Andrew will share with you when he's ready."

"Ha!" Enid shook her head. "You don't know him at all, do you? Andrew doesn't talk to anyone about his feelings. That's why we're all so surprised he's starting a grief support group. He keeps going on about how talking to that little girl helped him, so I suppose he has his reasons, but that's all he's telling any of us."

Enid eyed her. "Maybe you should talk to him. You have a way of getting him to open up."

"I'm probably the last person he wants to talk to. We've all pushed him enough. I think he needs to be left alone to figure out things for himself."

She should take her own advice. Maybe it didn't give her the answers she wanted, but at least she wouldn't be banging her head against the wall, either.

Enid looked like she was going to respond, but then Javier approached.

"Thank you again for the fresh herbs, Enid. Abuela will be so excited."

"I'm glad she can use them. Too many people don't know what to do with them, and I hate to see them go to waste."

Javier pointed at the package Enid held. "What's that? Something else to bring to Abuela?"

"No." Enid held it out to Layla. "Today is Layla's birthday, and I wanted to give her something to celebrate. And to thank her for everything she's done for us."

Layla accepted the package, staring at it. No one here knew it was her birthday. How could Enid, reputed to be the crankiest person in town, have been the only one to figure it out?

"It's your birthday? Why didn't you say something?" Javier turned to look at Layla.

She shrugged. "No one's ever made a big deal of it, so I didn't think to say anything."

Once she'd gotten beyond the childhood age of having birthday parties with her friends, Layla's parents had never done much for her birthday. In her friend circles, people had only celebrated milestones.

"That might have been before you came to Arcadia Valley, but not now," Javier said. "Not as part of the Quintana family. We celebrate birthdays, and they're a big deal. Who knows how many more you'll have."

Layla couldn't believe his words. Mostly because she used to dream about having a family like this. Not just for her birthday, but because she always thought they were a great excuse to get people together. "I'm not sure what to say."

Javier grinned. "You don't have to say anything. We're already having a barbecue at Abuela's tonight, and because their recital got canceled some of the girls are going to be showing us the Mexican dances they've learned. A birthday will make the evening even more special."

Though his offer sounded sincere, it seemed rude to intrude on their party.

"I don't want to crash your party," Layla said.

"There's no such thing as crashing a Quintana party. Everyone is welcome. Besides, now we have a reason to celebrate."

No one had ever gotten this excited over her birthday before. She looked down at the present in her hands. Since her mother had passed away, she hadn't even received a birthday gift.

"What can I bring to the barbecue?" Layla asked, determined to make happy new memories for her birthday.

"Nothing," Javier said, his face full of warmth. "There will be plenty of food, based on the way Abuela has been cooking. Molly was also whipping up something in the kitchen, and if I know the others, they'll bring just as much. Trust me. There will be more than enough."

Javier turned to Enid. "You and Andrew should come too. Abuela will want to thank you for the herbs. Plus, we have some friends who are forming a Mariachi band, and they are using our little barbecue as a chance to practice. I know how you like your Mariachi music."

Enid grinned, her smile splitting her face. "That I do. I haven't been out and gotten to hear good music in a long time. Do you need a cake?"

"While I'm sure there will be plenty of desserts, you're right. Layla needs a cake," Javier said.

Layla opened her mouth to protest, but Enid waved her away. "Don't you dare argue. Javier is right. Every year is a gift, and we should celebrate."

Then Enid turned, gesturing at Andrew, who was approaching.

"Don't you agree Andrew? It's Layla's birthday, and we need to celebrate."

Now this was definitely a conversation she didn't want to have. Andrew didn't need to be told how precious and short life was. And she really didn't want that discussion to involve her.

"Happy birthday, Layla. Why didn't you tell us sooner?"

"I didn't realize birthdays were such a big deal in Arcadia Valley." It was weird to have him acting so normally around her. She wasn't sure what to think of the ups and downs that seemed to go with every interaction she had with him.

"See?" Javier said. "It's decided. We will celebrate tonight at Abuela's. Enid is in charge of the cake, and you'll come too, won't you Andrew?"

The trapped look on Andrew's face was exactly what Layla had expected to see. Maybe the friendliness only came in front of other people because he didn't want anyone to question why he was acting so oddly.

"I was actually going to-"

Javier shook his head. "Don't you dare say work, my friend. You work too much, and you need to learn to relax a little. The work will keep. But this is a treasured time with friends, and you need to enjoy it. You were just telling me that you were wrong to shut yourself off from everyone. So if you meant what you said, you will come."

Andrew looked so uncomfortable, especially because he'd already made it clear he didn't want to be involved with her socially, and here he was, being forced into it.

"That's not necessary," Layla said. "Andrew has been working hard to reenter the world, and we can't expect him to completely change overnight. If he would rather work, then let him work."

She looked at Andrew, hoping he would understand she was giving him a way out. It wasn't fair to make him celebrate and participate in an event that would only make him miserable.

140

She'd already done more than enough to make him feel that way.

"I suppose I can come for little while," Andrew said, averting his gaze so he wasn't looking at her.

He was making it abundantly clear that he stood by everything he'd said about not being ready for her. She should be thankful at least that he wasn't making a scene, or letting everyone know what a fool she'd been. She couldn't imagine how humiliating it would be to have to face everyone with them knowing that she'd thrown herself at him and he'd rejected her. At least it was a good wake-up call and a warning to keep her from ever doing it again.

**

Andrew hated remembering the hurt expression on Layla's face. Even a few hours later as he left Demi's Delights, where Gram had sweet-talked them into making a short-notice birthday cake for Layla, he could still picture how hard she'd been trying to pretend he hadn't hurt her.

It didn't take a genius or expert in romance to know that he'd handled the situation badly. Kissing her had been such a shock that he still wasn't sure how to process it. He'd be lying if he said he didn't feel something. Maybe it had been too long since he'd kissed Mykel, but he couldn't remember a kiss ever moving him the way Layla's had. But when he thought about Mykel, his stomach hurt. What did it mean when you promised to love someone forever and found yourself having feelings for someone else? Was he a liar? Did he not know his own feelings? Or was he destined to be faithless in his commitments to others?

He'd hoped to have a chance to ask Ben about it, since Ben

was dating again after the death of his wife. How did he deal with the feelings of disloyalty?

But maybe those questions were too personal to ask a man he barely knew. It was one of the topics he hoped to explore in his support group. How did others handle the conflicting feelings that arose when you found yourself attracted to someone else?

And now he was forced to attend a party where he'd celebrate Layla and hopefully not make a fool of himself. He was avoiding her, and she probably knew it. He wanted to have a relationship with her, but felt conflicted over his loss. So it seemed wrong to spend time in her company. It felt like he was leading her on. No one liked playing those kind of games, and he was trying his best not to do so with Layla. He didn't know how to deal with these budding feelings in a fair way, when everything was so new to him.

When he arrived at Javier's grandmother's house, the party was already in full swing. The sounds of Mariachi performers warming up in the backyard had Gram's feet tapping. By the end of the night, a whole group of old ladies would probably be dancing like fools, and he would love every minute of it.

At least he hoped so. The unknown factor was how he was going to handle being there with Layla.

Andrew carried the cake over to the table where people had put desserts. Javier's estimation that there would be more than enough food had been correct. At this rate, they could invite the whole town and still have food left over. Everyone had brought something to share, and Andrew was going to have a hard time choosing what to eat.

He spotted Layla standing in a group of women, laughing

like she was having a great time. Good for her. She deserved to enjoy her birthday, especially since he'd basically done everything he could to ruin it.

What kind of man rejects a woman on her birthday?

But it was even worse to lead her on.

One of the other ladies must have noticed him watching them, because she whispered something to Layla, then Layla turned in his direction.

Clearly everyone knew they were in a strange situation.

Fortunately, he didn't have to say or do anything, because Allie came to stand beside him.

"I heard about what you said to Dad."

A no less difficult conversation than the one he'd have with Layla, but at least he had answers for Allie. She'd been working extra shifts since their father visited, and they hadn't had time to talk. At least talking to Allie would be a good distraction from Layla.

"He needs to back off," Andrew said. "We're all doing the best we can, and it would be a lot easier if he'd leave us alone."

She nodded slowly. "But he came all the way from Seattle to say it. Maybe he's right. Maybe I'm just wasting my life."

Andrew took her by the elbow. "Come with me."

She followed him to the edge of Javier's grandmother's yard, where, if you looked closely enough, you could see the lavender fields in the distance.

"You know what used to be the view? Cows. And the smell? How many times were we teased as kids because we smelled like cow manure? Now what does everything smell like?"

Allie smiled. "Lavender."

"And whose idea was that?"

The smile fell from his sister's face. "But we aren't making a lot of money. We lost the bid to supply that natural foods store because we aren't a big enough operation."

"So we try again. You can't give up because you've had a few setbacks. We all believe in you and your dream. Caroline is going to turn the place into a living history farm, where kids can come for day camps and learn about natural living, and adults can come stay and get in touch with their roots. And your lavender is going to be sold all over the world."

Allie shook her head. "I don't think so. That kind of carbon footprint would be a nightmare."

He gave her a playful nudge. "You know what I mean."

"Yeah, but Dad . . ."

He hated how discouraged his sister sounded. Poor Allie had spent her whole life trying to please their father, but Bart had dubbed her the Hot Mess Express because she was so scattered and disorganized. They'd had enough conversations about Allie's scatterbrained personality that Andrew knew his father believed none of Allie's plans would ever succeed.

Which was why Andrew did all he could to help her. He believed in Allie. She just needed a little help making it all happen.

"You know I'm here for you," Andrew said, putting his arm around her.

She rested her head on his shoulder. "I know. But at some point, you're going to want to live your own life. Maybe it's better I quit now instead of wasting everyone's time and money."

Looking down at her, Andrew said, "Stop that. I don't see it as a waste. Besides, this is my life. You're the creative genius, and I'm the guy who makes it all happen. In the corporate world, that's how it works. You've got someone handling the business plans and the finances, and someone else does what you're doing. It's what I did in Seattle. The only difference is that I'm working for a company I believe in."

Allie stepped aside and looked at him. "I thought you liked your job in Seattle?"

"I did, but being back home has reminded me that a man's life is more than a nice paycheck. This is where I belong."

The Mariachi music started up again, and they turned to the sound.

"We're always the party poopers, aren't we?" Allie said, sighing.

"I'm trying not to be, but . . ."

Andrew's eyes immediately alighted on Layla. It was like an instinct, always seeking her out first.

"What's the deal with you two, anyway?"

He shook his head, not looking at his sister. The one person in the world besides Mykel that he hadn't been able to hide his feelings from was Allie. Then he closed his eyes. No, that wasn't true. Layla could also read him like a book.

"She wants things I don't think I can give her. I don't know how to be with anyone besides Mykel, and . . ." Andrew let out a long sigh. "I don't want to hurt her. Layla's a really good person, and she deserves better than a messed-up guy who can't get over his dead fiancée."

Allie drew in an audible breath, the kind that always meant he was in for a good telling-off.

He brought his attention back to her.

"Don't you think that's for her to decide? Look, if she likes you despite all of your faults, including the fact that you're one of the most bone-headed dorks on the planet, don't you think you ought to give her a chance? It's not like you or I have a whole lot of people banging down the door to date one of the crazy Bigbys, so why not at least try?"

They had earned a certain reputation in high school that they'd never quite outlived. Though they each had their own circle of friends, most of their peers had thought them odd. And maybe they were a little odd. For a time, Andrew did have some of the cheerleaders chasing after him because they thought he was cute, but he'd never been interested. When he'd turned them down one too many times, they'd made sure everyone else thought he was a weirdo.

And maybe he was. What normal guy wouldn't want to go out with a girl like Layla?

"What if I do it all wrong," Andrew said, returning his attention to Allie. "I don't know what I'm doing with women. Mykel asked me out, she kissed me first, and she was the one who pushed me out of my shell. I mean, I always liked girls, but they made me feel so tongue-tied and stupid. Mykel saw beyond that, and loved me anyway."

Allie nodded slowly, like she understood completely. Which she should, since other than Javier she'd been his main confidant all these years.

"That sounds a lot like what Layla's doing to you, only you're pushing her away."

Andrew couldn't help chuckling. "Yeah, she even kissed me."

Allie gaped at him. "Are you serious? She kissed you? When? How? Why didn't you say anything? Did you kiss her back? Andrew, this is huge! You and Layla kissed!"

Even though he didn't feel much like laughing, he had to grin at his sister's exuberant response.

"Yes, I'm serious. She kissed me, and it was wonderful. Of course I kissed her back. I didn't want to say anything because I'm not the kind of guy to kiss and tell. I shouldn't have even told you."

Allie's eyes shone, and he shook his head. "But it's not going to happen again. I told her I wasn't ready, and I think I really hurt her feelings when she tried to get me to talk about it."

Disgust rolled over Allie's face. "Well, duh. Do you know the amount of courage it takes for a girl to kiss a guy? Like, a thousand times what it takes for a guy to kiss a girl. We have been taught from a very early age that we're supposed to wait for the guy to make a move. She put herself out there, and you totally shut her down."

It was just like his sister to verbally slap him with the truth. One of the things he liked about her, even if not everyone appreciated it.

"What was I supposed to do? Lead her on? Make her think I was totally in love with her when I'm still in love with Mykel? When I miss Mykel every single day?"

Although, if he was honest, he was starting to miss her less and less, especially when Layla was around.

Andrew let out a long sigh. "What if I hurt her? What if I can't give her what she needs?" He closed his eyes, realizing the deeper fear. "What if I end up getting hurt because I'm not the man she wants me to be?"

Giving him a sympathetic look, Allie put her arm around him again. "You mean, what if you fail?"

At Andrew's nod, Allie gave him a shove. "You idiot! That is exactly the fight we've been having about me. I'm not sure I want to go forward with my lavender business because, deep down, I'm scared that like everything else I've tried in my life, it will fail. But you keep pushing me, saying I shouldn't be scared, and I should keep trying. How is that any different from you being unwilling to date because you're afraid things won't work out?"

Zing. That one almost physically hurt, mostly because Allie was right. It was like every piece of advice he'd ever given her was invalidated because he was stuck in this pit of fear and pain that had developed after Mykel's death.

His sister glared at him. "If you're going to give up on love, then I'm giving up on my lavender business."

Most people would have seen it as an idle threat, but Andrew knew Allie well enough to know she was dead serious. She had a long history of cutting off her nose to spite her face. With her lavender business, she had a real chance of succeeding, if she'd only let herself.

His failure to pursue Layla would be a convenient excuse for Allie to quit.

"And if I give this thing with Layla a shot?"

Allie's glare intensified.

"You started it," he said. "Don't threaten me if you're not up to facing an equally difficult challenge."

His sister started laughing, and he joined in, like they always had when they both realized how ridiculous they were being.

"All right," she finally said, "I'll bite. I'll even talk to Dad the next time he drops by."

Her immediate negative response about their father reminded him of how because of Layla's influence Gram and Aunt Camille were getting along better. No, not just Layla's influence. He'd been the one to give Aunt Camille the advice to stop treating Gram like the enemy. Maybe it was time he took his own advice.

"Maybe we need to quit assuming the worst of him. Give him a chance. When we talked the other day, I let him know that things needed to change, and we have to stop seeing each other as adversaries."

Allie gave him an annoyed look. "And maybe you should tell that to him. Because the second he lays eyes on me, he lays into me."

Unfortunately, her words were true. Their father made accusations first, listened almost never.

"He did that to me too," Andrew said. "And I told him that I wanted to be his son, not his enemy. He backed off."

Andrew had managed to avoid him since, but that hadn't been an intention on Andrew's part. He'd been out running errands the past couple of times their father had stopped by.

"I can try it," Allie said grudgingly. "But if he so much as mentions me doing back to college . . ."

"Maybe you learn to respond with grace instead of yelling at him and running away."

Allie looked like he'd just felt when she'd hit him with the truth. But she needed to hear it. Because that was how things always went with them and their father. He'd make accusations, Allie would argue with him, they'd both fight without listening to the other person's side, until finally Allie ran off crying, and Andrew was left to pick up the pieces.

"He's just so unreasonable," Allie said, tears filling her eyes. "He never listens to me."

Once again, Andrew felt like the discussion was a reflection of his own life. He hadn't been reasonable with Layla, hadn't heard her out. Hadn't even given her the chance to listen to him and understand why he felt the way he did, and what his fears were.

"I think we both need to do more listening," Andrew said, looking back over at Layla.

At least she was having a good time. She didn't seem to notice that Andrew and Allie were off having their own private crises that in some way, Layla had sparked.

"You should tell her all the stuff you just told me," Allie said, coming alongside him and following his gaze. "Leave it to her to decide if a relationship with you is worth fighting for. She's already put herself out there more than most people would. You at least owe it to her to share your heart. What she does with it is up to her, but you at least tried."

He looked over at her. "I'm assuming that's your game plan with Dad."

"You know what they say about people when they assume. . ." Then she grinned. "But I suppose, in your case, when it comes to me, you're right."

Andrew smiled back. "No matter how he responds, or what he says, I'll be here for you. I love you no matter what."

Giving him another tiny shove, Allie said, "And if things don't work out with you and Layla, I'll bring home a gallon of ice cream and some chick flicks, and we can binge on them both."

"Chick flicks?"

"Yes." Allie gave him a satisfied grin. "If you mess this relationship up, then clearly you need an education about women. And there is no better way to learn about them than to watch the movies we love. With lots of popcorn covered in nutritional yeast."

Then she gave him a mischievous look. "In fact, you might want to watch a couple before talking to her. Because the whole, 'despite all of my objections' garbage didn't go so well for Mr. Darcy. It worked out in the end, but it sure made things harder."

Though he had no idea who this Darcy guy was, Allie did have a point. The biggest challenge Andrew faced in expressing his feelings to Layla was that she wouldn't understand.

But he had to try.

Chapter Twelve

As Layla watched the Grannies dance to Mariachi music, she couldn't help thinking this was the happiest she could ever remember being. Hands down, it was the best birthday she'd ever had.

Javier and his friends had made a bonfire, and the children were roasting marshmallows and making S'mores, even though they'd probably had more than their fill of dessert.

A shadow blocked the light from the fire, and Layla looked up.

Andrew.

He'd done a nice job of avoiding her the entire evening, which on one hand made her happy because it meant they wouldn't have another awkward conversation. But on the other hand, there was still a part of her that wished things weren't so weird between them.

"I hope you had a nice birthday," he said, looking just as uncomfortable as he had acted around her lately.

She wasn't going to let him rain on her parade. Not when she'd had such a wonderful evening.

"I did, thank you." She smiled at him, wishing she knew where this was going, and hoping that it wouldn't end in disaster-again.

"I, um . . ." He shifted, then looked over his shoulder. Layla followed his gaze and noticed Allie standing nearby, giving him what seemed like an encouraging look.

Layla wasn't sure what that meant. In some ways, she was afraid to hope or read too much into it. Hadn't she been burned enough, getting her hopes up?

"I haven't been fair to you," he said, returning his gaze to her. "You've tried to be open with me, and I've shut you out. I was afraid to talk to you tonight because I don't want to ruin your birthday, but I'm afraid if don't, I might chicken out. So . . . if you want to have that conversation I refused to have with you earlier, we can. Or, if you want to wait and do it on a different day, I promise, I will."

Layla's heart thudded so loudly, she wasn't sure she'd heard his words correctly. But Andrew closed his eyes, took a deep breath, then looked at her again.

"I'm scared, Layla. That's why I haven't talked to you. I'm afraid that when I tell you what's on my heart, and how little I feel I have to offer you, you'll reject me, and I'm going to get hurt."

She'd thought she'd seen Andrew vulnerable before. He'd certainly shared more of his heart with her than she'd seen him do with anyone else. Yet here he was, showing an even deeper side of himself. So deep that she hardly recognized him.

"I'm scared too," she said. "I really like you, and I've tried to be patient, and I'm trying to understand what you're going through. But what if I open myself to you and I can't live up to the legendary Mykel?"

Sympathy shone in his eyes, and he nodded slowly. "I don't make it easy on people, do I?"

"No, you don't."

He'd told her he didn't want to play games, and neither did she. Layla stood and gestured towards the garden.

"Why don't we take a walk so we can have this conversation without an audience?"

She already knew Allie was watching, probably to give him moral support. And others would notice them talking, and though she knew they cared about them, they'd be watching with their own interest. Whatever happened between her and Andrew, it needed to be between them.

Especially because Andrew was right. Neither of them knew how this conversation would go, and in the end, one or both of them could wind up hurt. She might have been prepared to compromise and take it slowly before, but as she watched all the couples who were newly married or newly engaged dancing to the Mariachi music, she was no longer willing to accept half measures. No more chasing someone who didn't want her.

If Andrew wanted to be with her, then he needed to be all in. Willing to do the work together to figure out what they both wanted. Willing to let her in as he dealt with his grief.

If he couldn't do that, then she was done trying.

They walked in silence as they passed happy people celebrating and enjoying the evening. Caroline waved at them, then Hayden grabbed her and pulled her into his arms and onto the dance floor.

Yes, Layla deserved that in her life.

And Andrew deserved it, too, even if he didn't know it yet.

When they finally arrived at the edge of Abuela's garden, Layla turned to him. "So what did you want to say?"

"I like you too," Andrew said, looking out over the fields. "Maybe more than like, I don't know."

He turned to her and let out a long sigh. "I'm afraid to spend more time with you exploring whatever this is because I don't want to lead you on. I don't know if this is the real thing, or if I'm just experiencing my first feelings of attraction since Mykel died."

Well, she'd asked for honesty. She supposed a declaration of love wasn't possible, but this seemed a little weak.

Andrew examined her face, making her feel more exposed than she'd allowed herself to be in a long time.

"I did the Mr. Darcy thing, didn't I?"

Layla stared at him. "What are you talking about?"

He shrugged. "According to Allie, there's this guy in a movie named Mr. Darcy who really messed up telling a girl how he felt, and it made their relationship even worse. I did that just now, didn't I?"

As wretched as he looked, Layla couldn't help chuckling a little. "It sounds like *Pride and Prejudice*. And yes, he did completely mess up the love declaration. So why did you just do it?"

Gesturing to a nearby bench, Andrew shook his head. "I don't know. Let's sit."

They sat for a few moments, neither one of them speaking. Though Layla was dying to ask all sorts of questions, she wanted him to be the one offering information, not her prying it out of him.

"I wasn't joking when I told you the other day that I didn't know what to do with women. Mykel is the only person I've ever dated."

Javier had told her that, but the way Andrew said it, he sounded almost ashamed.

"What's wrong with that?"

"Nothing." He let out a long sigh. "But I always feel awkward around women because I never know how to act or what to say. After Mykel died, there was a woman at church who was really nice to me. I thought we were friends, and that she was just offering me the comfort of a friend. I didn't realize that she'd developed feelings for me, and when I tried to clear up the misunderstanding, she accused me of leading her on."

The distress on Andrew's face was obvious. "It caused a lot of problems in our church. Even though Pastor Harris thought I didn't do anything wrong, a lot of people took her side. She ended up leaving the church, but not before she tried getting me kicked out of church and the pastor fired. The elder board even got involved. Obviously, her plan didn't work, but I can't help wondering how I could have done things differently."

His genuine sorrow over the situation made his initial declarations about friendship with women not seem so crazy. The last thing someone as sensitive as Andrew would have wanted would be to cause dissent in the church.

The look he gave her made her heart sink.

"I wouldn't do that," she told him. "People have relationships not work out all the time. It's no reason to cause trouble for someone else."

He wore a guilty expression as he turned to her again, leaning in slightly.

"I don't believe you would do any of those things, but I also worry about your feelings. I would never intentionally hurt anyone, especially you. Knowing that I don't have a good sense of how I come across, it just seems easier to keep my distance."

Though she could understand why he felt that way, it was also frustrating to see how it seemed to paralyze and prevent him from having any sort of relationship with a woman. Especially when he knew she wouldn't do that.

"If you know I wouldn't do that to you, then why the fear?"

The pained look on Andrew's face almost made her feel bad for making him go down that path. But he was right, if they were to have any future together, they had to be able to talk about difficult topics. Layla scooted closer to him on the bench, hoping he'd see it as a sign of encouragement.

"The thing I feel the worst about with that situation is that I think she was truly hurt by my actions. She genuinely believed we had a future, even though I didn't see how I'd done anything to make her think that. How can I have conversations with you that are clearly romantic in nature, not being sure I can commit to you?"

Maybe he really was as clueless as he'd claimed. "People who date do it all the time."

He gave her a funny look, and Layla remembered that he'd already told her he didn't date much. A fact Javier had confirmed in his earlier conversations with her.

But that didn't let him off the hook. "So instead of taking a chance, you've been running away?"

Greene County Library
120 N. 12th St.
Paragould, AR 72450

Andrew nodded. "Now that both you and Allie have said it, it sounds really stupid. In my defense, when it comes to you, I don't know how to think rationally."

"You could have fooled me." Layla smiled at him, hoping to lighten the atmosphere. "Even though some of your arguments about your grandmother's care were a little ridiculous, you also said a lot of things that made sense. I think that's one of the things I've always respected about you. You're very wise. At least when you don't let your emotions take over."

"That's the trouble," he said. "When it comes to people I care about, I can't seem to think rationally. At least not until it's too late."

"You seem to be doing a fine job of thinking rationally now, so either you're not as bad as it as you say, or you don't care about me."

Even though she'd been telling everyone to back off and not push so hard, she was starting to realize that the more she showed him just how ridiculous his fears and arguments were, the more he saw it too.

But was it enough?

She'd moved closer to him during their conversation, and he hadn't seemed to be scared of her or even scooted away. Surely it meant she was getting her message across.

"I do care about you, that's the trouble. Part of me is so scared of messing things up with you because I truly value having you in my life. You said earlier that I made you a better nurse. I think you make me a better person. What if we pursue something romantic, and I end up hurting you?"

The problem with every human relationship. "There are no

guarantees. Besides, we all hurt one another from time to time. Even in the best relationships. We don't mean to, but we're all human and we all make mistakes. The question is, how well do we forgive one another after we've made those mistakes?"

She liked the thoughtful expression on his face, as if he was considering her words, and trying to see how he could apply them to his life.

"I think you and I do a good job a forgiving one another," she said. "If you look back on all of our disagreements, the one thing they all have in common is that when we both had time to cool down, we ended up talking about it, and it made our relationship stronger. I think that's what is supposed to happen in all relationships."

Andrew nodded slowly, and she couldn't help respecting him on a deeper level for sharing the parts of his heart that he'd probably never shared with anyone else.

"It's a risk, being open with others," she said, taking his hand. "You risk rejection, but you also risk missing out on something really wonderful. I was just thinking earlier that you and I both deserve to have wonderful things in our lives. Whether that's together or apart, I don't know, but I'd like to think it's worth a try."

When he didn't answer at first, she wondered if she'd pushed too hard again. Asked for too much. But then she shook her head slowly. No, it wasn't too much. If he wasn't willing to give it to her, then it just meant he wasn't the right one for her.

She closed her eyes, and briefly asked God to help her live with whatever answer Andrew gave.

Andrew squeezed her hand, and she turned to look at him.

He smiled at her. "You're willing to take me as I am, with no guarantees of the future?"

"None of us has guarantees. Surely you've figured that out by now." Layla turned her body even more to look at him. "I don't mean to dig into your pain, but I want you to think about something. If, when you'd met Mykel, you'd known how things would end, would you have avoided a relationship with her?"

Though she'd meant it as something for him to consider, not answer, Andrew shook his head. "Absolutely not. I treasure that time, even though we had so little of it."

"Then why not treasure the time you have with every other person in your life? We're all going to die, so why spend the life we have living in fear of it?"

Andrew chuckled as he squeezed her hand again. "You've clearly been hanging out with Mona."

She liked the feel of his hand in hers, liked how the longer they touched the more comfortable he started to act.

"I've been a nurse for a lot of years. A lot of patients have died. It's part of life."

He examined her face, as though he was trying to look deeper into her heart.

"Thank you for being patient with me."

She smiled at him, but the heaviness in her heart told her that she needed more.

"I can be patient. But we can't have this conversation and then you go back to your hiding game. When we leave here, it's as a couple, or it's not. And once we decide to be a couple, if we decide to be done, we're done. I won't do the up and down, back and forth thing. I've been there, and it isn't fair."

The air grew still as he appeared to be pondering her words. Weighing them. Deciding just how much he was willing to give. Good.

"Tell me about him," Andrew said. "You know my past, what's driving you here?"

It felt like all the oxygen had been sucked out of her lungs at his words. She should have been prepared for his question. After all, he had been open with her. But she hadn't expected the way her heart suddenly ached at having to be so vulnerable.

Maybe they both needed vulnerability lessons.

Layla took a deep breath. "Actually, there are two hims. Or maybe more."

She looked back over Abuela's farm, the people mingling, the scent of Mexican food in the air.

"I came to Arcadia Valley to get in touch with my roots. When my parents got married, my dad told my mom it was him or her family. She chose him. He hates being Mexican, hates how some people are prejudiced against us, so he's done everything he can to be fully American. My mother did it to go along with him, but growing up, I always sensed an unhappiness in her, a longing."

Even now, Layla could picture her mother's sadness. The way she'd looked when she'd seen any reminder of the life she'd left behind.

"I had that same longing, and I wanted to know about my Mexican heritage. But Dad said that if I 'went Mexican' on him, I was no longer his daughter."

She shook her head and looked at Andrew. "I can relate to your family problems. In my case, I spent years trying to please my father, trying to be enough for him. Chasing him to make him love me. But when I told him I'd contacted Abuela, he gave me a choice-be a Mexican or be his daughter. It's been several years, and we haven't spoken since."

She swallowed, blinking back tears as she thought about how even now she sometimes wondered if there was a way she could get him to understand her choices and learn to love her anyway. He'd made it clear he didn't want a Mexican daughter, but something in her still wanted him.

Some time while she was speaking, Andrew had put his arm around her and drawn her close to him. He smelled of all the masculine things one would expect, but there was also a hint of lavender.

She looked up at him and smiled. Being in Andrew's arms felt safe. Like she didn't have to worry about anything.

"Every relationship I've had with men since then has been me chasing them. The more a guy didn't want me, the more interested I was. I suppose I'm lucky I didn't end up in an abusive situation."

Taking a deep breath, Layla continued. "My last boyfriend was Troy. He was incredible in a lot of ways. Except that he was never as committed to the relationship as I was. I was helping him recover after a car accident. After a few months, I realized he was dependent on his pain pills. I tried to get him help, but he wasn't interested. The drugs owned him, and the more I tried to help, the more he pushed me away. When we finally broke up, I blamed myself. Especially because a couple months later, he overdosed and died."

She hadn't realized she'd started crying until she felt Andrew press her head to his shoulder and noticed that she made his shirt wet. He kissed the top of her head.

"And here you are, chasing another man you think doesn't want you," he said quietly.

Layla looked up at him, surprised at how succinctly he'd summed up her life. And their relationship.

"I want you, Layla. I want you so much that it scares me. Scares me that I won't be enough for you, and that I can't move beyond my past enough to give you what you need."

Tears filled his eyes. "But mostly I'm scared that if I could have feelings like this for someone else, what does this mean for how I felt about Mykel? If I can fall out of love with her, what if I fall out of love with you? I care too much about you to hurt you, and I don't know how to do this right."

She wrapped her arms around him and hugged him tight. "We just do the best we can."

He kissed the top of her head again. "Then I'm all in. Whatever this is, we're going to figure it out together."

She looked up at him, and then he bent down and kissed her like a man who meant it.

Chapter Thirteen

The first meeting of his men's grief support group didn't go as well as Andrew had planned. Despite all of his invitations and talking to people like Ben, the only person who'd shown up was Andrew.

Pastor Harris poked his head into the room. "Not a lot of takers?"

"Nope. The counselor even cancelled at the last minute."

The pastor came into the room, grabbed a cookie off the plate, and took a bite. "Not bad. Allie must not have made these."

"No, Gram did, using one of the diabetic recipes from the new health group she and her friends formed."

"They're really good. I'm pleased to see how many people in the church have been participating in all of the healthy living activities. It seems like Arcadia Valley is becoming a hub for health."

Andrew sighed. "Except for mental health, when it comes to grief. Even McKenna ditched me for horseback riding."

Pastor Harris chuckled. "I'm sure most people would rather be riding a horse than talking about their feelings. You included."

"True." Andrew looked around the room, trying to picture all the people he knew would benefit from this group, but the pastor was right. Everyone had more important things to do than talk about their grief.

"How have your personal counseling sessions been going?" The pastor sat down next to him.

"Good. I'm learning a lot about facing my fears and finding healthy ways to deal with my grief. But sometimes I still feel stuck on a lot of my questions."

"Like what? Maybe I can help."

Pastor Harris sounded so sincere in his request, and he'd been one of the people Andrew had pushed away. Especially after the whole elder board incident.

One of the things he'd been trying to do was make amends for all of his bad behavior.

"First, you can let me apologize. I know I shut you out. And I distanced myself after all the to-do where you nearly lost your job. I was afraid that you'd be hurt even more."

For a moment, Pastor Harris was silent, then he looked at Andrew as though he, too, had some things to get off his chest. "I didn't realize that you'd taken the situation so personally. John Everett was upset because I didn't hire Bethany as our children's ministry leader. She wasn't qualified. I was also concerned that she'd been spreading rumors about you. John did everything he could to get back at me, and I didn't realize how it affected everyone else. I was sorry to see you leave your ministry positions. A lot of people quit, and it's taken time to rebuild. I always thought I'd done something wrong in how I handled it, but the remaining elders have assured me that it was simply John throwing a tantrum because he didn't get what he wanted. Just like Bethany did to you when you rejected her advances."

The pastor looked at him with sympathy. "I'm sorry for not being more proactive in making sure you were all right after it all happened. I thought once John packed up his family and moved to Oregon that the matter was settled. I should have talked to you about it."

"And I thought my actions had caused the trouble. I was trying to be helpful by removing myself from the situation."

After his conversations with Layla, Andrew realized he hadn't done his share of talking, either. Once again, it seemed that he'd made a lot of assumptions without getting to the bottom of the situation.

"I guess we're both at fault, then. Not talking about things seems to be a common problem these days."

The pastor gestured around the room. "Hence, why no one showed up. Men especially struggle with sharing our feelings, but we could all benefit from it from time to time. Don't give up on your mission. I think you're right to want to help others, but you'll find that the way you do it changes over time. I know that's how it's been for me."

Something about the advice rang true in Andrew's head, making him think about the way he'd been approaching his grief.

"Is it wrong that I'm trying to do something productive with my pain? Is this just another way I'm hiding from it?"

The pastor smiled. "Judging by the way you were holding hands with Layla at church this week, I think you've stopped hiding. We're shaped by our experiences, so it's only natural that you'd want to do something good with Mykel's death."

Layla's name automatically brought a smile to Andrew's face. Only a few months before, the thought of romance would have made him break out in hives. But he wouldn't have been able to make all these changes without Layla's love and support.

Of course, none of these changes would have happened without Layla pushing him, either, but he was happy she'd been willing to stick with him even though he'd been such a jerk.

"Do you think it's weird that I'm dating after Mykel's death?"

The question popped out of Andrew's mouth before he could think about it.

"No. I think a lot of us are pleased to see you so happy. I only met Mykel a couple of times when you came to visit, but she seemed like the kind of person who'd want you to be happy as well."

That's what everyone said, and he wanted to believe it, but he still couldn't get past his guilt.

"What does it say about my faithfulness if I promised to love her forever, and now I'm starting to feel that way about someone else?"

The pastor appeared to think for a moment, then got up and picked up one of the Bibles from the back table. He handed it to Andrew.

"Do me a favor and read John 3:16."

Andrew stared at him. "I memorized it as a kid. I don't need to read it."

"Humor me."

Flipping open the Bible, Andrew did as asked.

Pastor Harris nodded slowly. "Now, can you find where it says, 'Except Andrew Bigby,' or anyone else?"

"It doesn't." Andrew shook his head.

"So God, loved the entire world so much that he chose to sacrifice His son? No exceptions. Everyone. Given that we're made in the image of God, what do you think that says about the capacity of the human heart to love?"

Andrew chuckled. "It's pretty big, but I'm not capable of loving the whole world."

"But do you think you could love more than one woman?"

"I hope you're not encouraging polygamy," Andrew said, laughing. "But I get your point. If I can love Mykel, I can love someone else. I could love Layla."

A knock sounded at the door, and Ben poked his head in. "Sorry I'm late, but I got held up at Corrina's Cupboard. I heard what you said about God's love, and even though I probably missed everything else, I'm glad I caught that part. It's really helpful."

Andrew smiled at him as he entered the room. "I'm glad you came. And I'm glad you found something helpful. To be honest, I was hoping to talk to you about what it was like to be dating after your wife's death. I was just telling the pastor I feel guilty because I promised Mykel I'd love her forever, and here I am, thinking about loving someone else."

A knowing look crossed Ben's face as he sat in a nearby chair. "I understand that struggle. What the pastor said is true. We have the ability to love a limitless number of people if we let ourselves. Like you, I closed myself off. But now that I have Evelyn and Maisie in my life, I see what I was missing out on by not letting anyone in. I still miss Corrina and Zoey, and I'll never stop loving them, but there's still room to love a new family."

He paused slightly, then added, "It might sound like one of those trite sympathy things everyone says, but I know they wanted me to move on with my life and be happy. Being miserable won't bring them back, but at least I can honor them by living a full and happy life."

Andrew had heard all this before, but it was more helpful hearing it from someone who'd walked in his shoes.

In his shoes.

The pastor was right to think that Andrew's ministry had some changing to still do. But at least now, he knew what he was going to call it.

In fact, the idea started spinning in his mind so quickly, Andrew wasn't sure he totally had a grasp on it.

"What if I went back to school to get a counseling degree so I could help other men? Not just what we're doing here, because you're right, men don't want to get in a room and share their feelings with other men. But one on one? With a man who's been there?"

"I think you're on to something," Ben said. "I went to a counselor once, but I walked out as soon as I asked her if she'd ever lost a spouse and she said no."

Andrew nodded. "That's exactly how I've felt when people keep telling me what I should or shouldn't do with Mykel gone. It's part of why it was easier to isolate myself rather than have to deal with all their pithy but well-meaning comments."

"And that is progress," the pastor said. "At least now you recognize they were well-meaning. Getting a counseling degree is a great idea. I have some connections with a couple of colleges, so if you go that route, let me know and I can help."

Everyone kept telling him he needed to do something with his life after Mykel's death, and he'd thought that working on the farm was it. But now that he'd seen how he could use the tragedy to turn it into something that would help others, he finally knew what he needed to do.

He could still work on the farm, and it would still fill a part of his life that nothing else could, but now he understood how he was part of something bigger.

"I will, thank you. I need to go talk to Layla to see what she thinks. No matter which direction I take, I hope I can take it with her."

The pastor smiled at him. "And I think you also have your answer about loving her. It sounds like you're on the right track."

Turning to Ben, the pastor said, "Since we've wrapped up here, I'm hoping you have some time to sit down and tell me a little more about Corinna's Cupboard. Many of our small groups do service projects in the community, and if you're looking for more helpers, I think it would be a good fit."

"That would be great, thanks. I have quite a few ideas of how your small groups can get involved in our community." Ben turned and looked at Andrew. "It's amazing how so many individual tragedies bring us all together to do something bigger than any of us ever thought. Keep me updated on your plans, and let me know if I can help in any way."

Andrew nodded. "I will."

**

Layla practically fell into one of the booths at El Corazon. Javier already had some guacamole on its way, and while she didn't quite agree with Andrew's assessment that guacamole fixed everything, he was pretty close.

It had been a long day at work, and she had some of the most demanding patients. None of whom had any of the endearing qualities that made Enid grow on her, and one of whom reminded her way too much of her father.

She closed her eyes and sat back against the seat. She and Andrew had spent every evening together in the two weeks since her birthday, and while she generally looked forward to seeing him, she was so tired that she hoped his grief support group ran late so she could just go home and fall into bed.

"Long day?" Andrew's voice jolted her.

"I thought you were at your grief support group." She tried not to sound disappointed because even though her early bedtime plans were quickly going south, seeing his face lightened her load.

"No one came."

He slid into the chair across from her.

"I'm sorry, that's rough. I know you were really looking forward to it."

Andrew didn't look disappointed, though. Instead, he smiled. "I was, but I had a good talk with the pastor, and then Ben stopped by and gave me some wisdom."

He reached across the table for her hands, and she put them out to hold his.

"I love you, Layla. I was worried that it meant there was something wrong with me, because how could I love someone when I'd already given my heart away? But the pastor and Ben reminded me that God's love is limitless, and since we're made in God's image, we can love more than one person. There's still a lot I need to do in life, things that are important, but I want to do them with you by my side."

Before Layla could answer, Javier appeared at the table with a bowl of guacamole. "I see you won't be needing this after all."

Layla turned and glared at him. "Really?"

"Well, you came in because you were down, and now that Andrew has finally come to his senses and realized that you're the best woman he's going to find, you don't need cheering up."

Andrew gave his friend a look that Layla would have thought menacing if she hadn't known better.

"Give the lady her guac. And bring something for the gentleman. Then give us some privacy."

With a flourish, Javier set the guacamole on the table. Then he gave a mock salute. "As you wish."

Andrew chuckled as he shook his head. "I guess I shouldn't have told you that I love you in the middle of your family's restaurant."

Her heart felt warm and full. "But I'm glad you told me." She reached for his hands again. "It's been a long, hard day, and now it doesn't seem so bad."

The way he looked at her made the rest of her troubles seem almost like a bad dream. It hadn't been, but it seemed more bearable.

"Tell me what happened."

A simple gesture, but something in it nearly brought Layla to tears. Troy had never asked, and she'd always just launched into the conversation. As for her father, he'd also never cared.

Layla relayed the events of her day, down to the cranky man

who reminded her of her father.

"He had the nerve to ask me if I was legal," Layla said, finishing her tirade. "Legal or not, I'm still the one cleaning his leg wound. The whole reason I'm there is to take care of him, but he's so busy worrying about my documentation that he'd rather die. It was like trying to talk to my father."

The more she thought about the man, the more her calm disappeared. Though she'd already spoken with her boss, and he'd agreed that the patient had been inappropriate and would be assigned a different nurse, it still rankled that people could act like that.

Admittedly, much of her anger was about her father, but she'd forgotten that there were people like him out there.

Andrew gave her hand a squeeze. "That sounds terrible, I'm sorry. If there's something you need from me to make you feel better, let me know. But that brings up one of the things I wanted to talk to you about."

"Just having someone listen helped. Thank you."

Then the last few words he'd said rolled in her head. "What did you want to talk to me about?"

He hesitated, then said, "We're both struggling with the pain from our pasts. I talked to Pastor Harris today, and he told me that what happened with that girl wasn't my fault. It had never been about me, but about something completely different. I had built up all this fear because of my own perceptions of what had happened. I did that to some extent with Gram and her treatment because of what happened with Mykel. You taught me a lot about reconciliation."

He looked as though the words almost physically hurt him to

speak. It was hard to have sympathy for him though, considering he'd already asked her to do something quite painful for her.

"I was a jerk to a lot of people after Mykel's death," he said. "I've done my best to make reparations, and it feels good to know that a lot of my relationships are better than ever. But the thing I can't get out of my mind is the fact that I said a lot of ugly things to Mykel's doctor. I called him a murderer, and a lot of other horrible things. I was full of anger and I took it out on everyone around me. I want to apologize to him."

For a moment, it seemed almost as though everything stood still, though Andrew was still talking. Did he realize how important this was? And for him to include her in this process.

His words of love weren't just words, but he was putting action behind them.

"There's still a lot I need to do before we can take our relationship to the next level. I know I said I love you, and I do. I don't want life to pass us by without my having expressed the depth of my feelings for you. But I'm only just starting to realize the man I'm going to be without Mykel, and I don't know if he's going to be a man you can love."

All the hope Layla had been feeling shattered like fine porcelain on a cement floor. Troy had given her a similar Dear Jane speech, telling her that he needed to figure out who he was before he could commit to her.

"I see," she said, not bothering to hide the coldness from her tone as she pulled her hand away from his.

"I don't think you do." Andrew looked confused. "You care for me now, for who I am now. Will you still feel the same way when I don't need fixing anymore?"

The question made her feel sick to her stomach, so she pushed away the guacamole, which had just been so comforting to her. Now it smelled like something threatening to destroy her peace.

A pained expression filled Andrew's face. "We're broken people, Layla. Both of us. I need to be fixed, and you like to do the fixing. That's why you're a nurse. But you need the healing just as much as I do. We've spent a lot of time talking about my family issues, but not about yours. Cleary from the way you're upset over a man who reminds you of your father, you've still got to deal with those issues."

And clearly, he had no idea what he was talking about. Hadn't she dealt with it?

"So what are you saying?" She leaned forward, staring at him. "Are you saying we don't have a future because of my conflict with my father?"

"No." Andrew looked perplexed. "I'm just saying that what's the good in me doing all this work if you're not willing to do it for yourself? You push, and you tell everyone else that they have to work on reconciliation, but you aren't pursuing that path in your own life."

Then he sighed. "And yes, I am a little afraid that once you don't see anything else in me to fix that you aren't going to be interested anymore."

Part of her wanted to comfort him and tell him she would still care about him, no matter what. But the other part of her wanted to smack him for being so dense. And yet, she also felt this deep tearing at her insides over his accusations about her father.

He'd been the one to abandon her, not the other way around. True, she'd left, but only after he'd given his ultimatum.

What did Andrew know about her and her father?

And then, the look of sympathy he gave her turned those torn-up insides to mush.

This is what she'd done to him.

"I can't pretend to know what it's like to have your dad reject your identity," Andrew said. "But, when we're ready, if we decide to move in that direction, I'd like to be able to ask for his daughter's hand in marriage. I know it's hard, but can you reach out to him? I'll be there with you every step of the way."

Andrew looked across the table at her, his eyes full of sympathy over knowing what he was asking of her.

"Our future just can't be about fixing all the things wrong with me. I've learned a lot, and I'm willing to grow, but you have to be willing to do the same."

The wise-old-man look she remembered from when she first met him returned to his face, but this time, he looked even wiser. Like the changes he'd been making of late had impacted him on a much deeper level than she'd suspected.

"I challenged Allie to work on her relationship with our dad. You were there at our last encounter. I've come to realize that I need to keep trying, just as you did with me. I know my parents were hurt when I shoved them away after Mykel's death. My dad didn't agree with any of my decisions at that time."

The look he gave her made much of the uneasiness she'd been feeling go away. So full of love and trust, it made her feel warm all over, like they were a team. Yes, he was asking almost the unthinkable of her, but it seemed like a deeper commitment to reconciliation was what they all needed.

"My dealings with you taught me that even when it seems we're on completely different sides, most of the time we want similar things," Andrew said. "Sometimes we just see different ways of getting them. Deep down, I know my dad wants me to be happy. He thinks I'm going about it the wrong way. As for your dad, I'd like to think that he wants your happiness as well. Maybe he faced a lot of men like that ugly patient you had today, and he didn't want that for you. So he thought that the best way to handle it would be to make you lose your heritage. I don't know. I'm just tossing out an idea. We won't know until we ask."

Back to her father again.

Layla shook her head. "You don't know what he's like."

"No, I don't. But have you approached him with the view that he's anything but the monster you paint him as? If you'd told me a few months ago that Gram and Aunt Camille would be on friendly terms, I'd have laughed in your face. But all it took was for Camille to look at Gram a little differently."

How could she argue with that? Especially when Layla had seen the transformation for herself.

Frankly, if anyone but Andrew had told her those things about her father, she would've gotten up and walked away. Given all the pushing she'd done with him, it seemed like he'd earned the right to do so with her. And maybe, just as she had been with him, he might have a point.

"All right. We can talk to him. But I want you to know that this is a one-shot deal. I'll go and talk to him and give him one last chance, but I will not spend the rest of my life begging him to love me. I've done that, and I've moved on."

Even though she'd thought she had moved on, it felt good to feel the finality of her statement. She could make that one last attempt at reconciliation, then be able to firmly put her father in the past so she could continue with her future.

Andrew nodded. "Fair enough. I agree that you shouldn't spend the rest of your life chasing him, but I hope that we can find closure in a way that doesn't have you upset whenever you're reminded of him."

We. Because Layla was no longer alone. Even though she didn't hold out any hope that things with her father would get better, it felt good to know that she at least had Andrew by her side.

Chapter Fourteen

It was weird to be back in Seattle after all these years away, even weirder to be walking down the street holding hands with Layla. He never would have imagined this. It felt wrong, but only in the sense that Seattle didn't feel right to him anymore. While his time in Seattle had been good, he belonged in Arcadia Valley.

When they entered the doctor's office, Andrew was glad they'd called ahead to make an appointment. Layla had done all the talking and making arrangements, which was probably a good thing, because the last words Andrew had had with Dr. Wiggins hadn't been nice. He'd been afraid the doctor wouldn't see him at all.

The woman at the front desk seemed to know what was going on without a lot of explanations because she didn't make them wait but led them into an office.

Dr. Wiggins walked in, looking older and more tired than Andrew had remembered.

"Please, have a seat," Dr. Wiggins said.

They sat, and even though Andrew had rehearsed what he was going to say dozens of times since he and Layla had made the decision to come here, his tongue felt so thick in his mouth he couldn't form the words.

Dr. Wiggins spoke first. "I was surprised to receive Layla's phone call. I'm sorry to hear that the loss has been so hard on you."

Andrew took a deep breath as he finally found the words. "Thank you. I didn't realize how much it was holding me back, and I wouldn't have, except for Layla." He took her hand and squeezed it.

"What can I do for you?"

In all of his imaginings of how the apology would play out, he'd thought it would be harder. But looking at this tired man, Andrew felt so much sympathy for him that he knew he needed to do this. "I just wanted to tell you face-to-face that I'm sorry for how I treated you when Mykel died. I made a lot of angry and nasty accusations, and it wasn't right. You were doing the best you could as a doctor, and even though I wanted to blame you and find all the things I thought you were doing wrong, I know that wasn't fair."

"Thank you," Dr. Wiggins said. "We try not to take those words personally because we know that a person in pain says a lot of terrible things. It's hard to see someone you love go so quickly, so soon. I reviewed the case notes before you came, just in case I can think of anything that might help you in your grief. All I can say is that we did all we could for her. She knew she was going to die, and her only hope was that her death could be used to help others."

This was the first Andrew had heard of Mykel's wishes. "What do you mean?"

The doctor pinched the bridge of his nose, shaking his head slowly. "There was never a chance she was going to survive. Her cancer was too advanced, and the only thing we could do was buy her time. She asked for the experimental treatment, telling us that her body was no good to her anymore, but if it could be used to find things that would help others, to keep them from suffering, then she wanted to do it. Since you were listed in her records as being authorized to have her medical information, I assumed you knew."

He hadn't known. Mykel had never told him. All this time, he'd been blaming the doctor, when it was Mykel herself who'd made this decision.

"No, she didn't tell me. I didn't realize that the goal wasn't to cure her cancer, but to see if the drug would cure someone else's. I just remember reading a few months after her death that the investigational drug had been pulled from trials because it was linked to patient deaths."

Dr. Wiggins nodded slowly. "It's true they pulled the drug. We had such high hopes. And even though the drug didn't work, we learned a lot from Mykel's case."

Tears filled Andrew's eyes as he thought about how the sacrifice exactly illustrated the kind of person Mykel had been. He only wished she had told him. But maybe she'd tried. Whenever she talked negatively about the future or spoke about her impending death, Andrew would tell her not to be so pessimistic. He would encourage her and tell her that they were going to beat it, that she was going to live. But she'd faced the truth far sooner than he had. And rather than looking weakly at her fate, she decided to do something with it to help others.

"Thank you so much for telling me all of this," he told Dr. Wiggins. "You have no idea how much this means to me."

Then he looked over at Layla and smiled at her. "To my future. I have all the answers I need, and I'm grateful that you are able to take time out of your busy day to talk to me."

They all stood, and Andrew reached out to shake Dr. Wiggins' hand. Dr. Wiggins gave him a firm squeeze, then leaned forward and patted him on the shoulder. "I understand your loss. Both my wife and daughter died of the same cancer Mykel had, and it's fueled my career all these years. We may not have a cure yet, but thanks to a lot of generous people, we're getting closer."

Once again, Andrew found himself wishing he hadn't been such, as Allie would say, a bonehead. He was grateful that Layla had stood by him and not let his fears prevent his grandmother from getting the treatment she needed. He'd based so many of his actions on a wrong assumption. But as he and Layla exited the building, he felt a new sense of hope, knowing that he was at least taking steps to correct the error of his ways.

**

All roads led to Seattle, or at least it seemed that way to Layla. Her father was living in an apartment downtown, a fact which she shouldn't have learned about her parent by looking him up online. But, given that they'd already made arrangements to visit Seattle to talk to Dr. Wiggins, it seemed like a sign that she was supposed to visit her father.

However, the sinking feeling in her gut told her that it was a fool's errand to try to make peace with him. He clearly didn't want to have anything to do with her. Otherwise, he would've let her know he'd moved. But as they stood outside the glamorous apartment building, so fancy it had a doorman, trying to decide what to do, Layla had half a mind to tell Andrew to just forget it.

But as she started to turn away, she recognized a man walking towards the building. Her father. Andrew was looking at something on his phone, so he hadn't noticed. And even though he wore a nice suit, and had his hair slicked back in a new style, she knew it was him. And as he drew closer, it was clear he recognized her too.

"Layla?"

"Hi Dad."

Andrew put his phone away, and put his arm around Layla. "You must be Mr. Avila," Andrew said, holding out his hand. "I'm Andrew Bigby. It's a pleasure to meet you."

Layla's father looked at them suspiciously. "What can I do for you?" he asked.

"I was hoping we could talk," Layla said, trying to keep her voice steady.

"Here?"

Andrew gestured towards the building. "We could go inside your apartment to keep our words private."

Layla's father shook his head. "That's not possible. I don't have time to talk right now, but here's my card. You can call my secretary and set up an appointment."

As Layla's father handed Andrew his business card, Layla felt sick. How could a man who hadn't seen his daughter in years dismiss her so quickly? And with a business card?

A dark look crossed Andrew's face as he shoved the card into his pocket without even looking at it. "You mean to tell me that you don't have five minutes to speak with your daughter? She's come all the way from Idaho just to see you, to try to make amends, and you're brushing her off like you would a used-car salesman?"

Andrew shook his head. "I'm trying very hard not to judge, because I don't know you, and I know nothing about you. Help me understand why you would turn away your own daughter."

Layla tugged at Andrew's hand, hoping he would just leave it alone. Her father hated scenes, and if this went on much longer, it would become one. Besides, she'd spent too much of her life begging for his affection to make Andrew do it on her behalf. He clearly wasn't interested, and it was time they faced that fact.

Her father stared at Andrew like he was trying to figure him out. Finally, he said, "Fine. I'll give you five minutes. But you're right. This is no place for the conversation. I suppose you can come up to my apartment."

They followed Layla's father up to his apartment, and the closer they got, the more nervous she felt. When he opened the door, Layla was surprised at how sterile the place looked. Like a show home that no one lived in. Nothing personal to indicate her father was a human being. Certainly no pictures of Layla or her mother.

"My wife will be home soon, and I'd rather you not be here when she gets home."

Layla couldn't even process that new information. Her father had remarried and hadn't even talked to her about it? More and more, she was beginning to think this whole trip had been a waste of time. Her earlier conviction about needing to speak with him suddenly held no weight.

"Congratulations," Layla said quietly. "I hope you two are very happy."

Andrew gave her hand another squeeze, as if he knew how much those words hurt her to say them.

"Thank you," her father said. "Cynthia is a lovely woman, and she makes me very happy. I know it's hard for you to think about me having another wife, but your mother is gone, and I deserve to be happy."

His defensive tone made Layla almost feel bad for being angry that he'd remarried without telling her.

Though he seemed to be putting on the attitude of being strong, she could see where he was afraid. Maybe her opinion did matter to him after all.

"Of course you have the right to be happy. Mom is gone, and it would be silly for you to spend the rest of your life pining away for her."

Layla looked over at Andrew, wondering if would be appropriate to share anything personal about him. Andrew smiled.

Then he turned to her father and said, "It's hard to consider remarrying after a beloved spouse's death. But burying yourself with her doesn't do anyone any good. I can't imagine anyone would judge you for remarrying."

Her father's expression softened, like he was relieved that it wasn't going to be a fight about his new wife. He gestured to the sofas.

"You can sit down if you like. I don't have much to offer you for refreshment, maybe some water, but I'm happy to get it."

He seemed so uncomfortable that Layla didn't want to trouble him. It already seemed like a big deal for him to invite them in, and now to offer them a seat. Part of her still wanted to run away and forget the whole thing. But Andrew tugged at her hand and walked towards the couch.

Then Andrew smiled at her father. "That would be wonderful, thank you."

Her father nodded. "Of course."

When he went into the kitchen, Layla turned to Andrew and glared at him. What was he thinking, imposing further on her father's hospitality? He clearly didn't want them there, and taking advantage of the water offer seemed to only prolong it. Hadn't he seen enough? But Andrew gave her hand a squeeze, then let it go as her father returned, carrying three bottles of water.

"Is this all right?"

"Perfect, thanks." Andrew smiled at him. "I know you have other things to do, so we won't impose too much on your time. We're here for two reasons. Number one, Layla and I have embarked upon a journey to heal our past relationships. And number two, our own relationship is becoming serious, and I think it's important to know one another's families."

Layla hadn't been expecting him to be so blunt. But her father seemed to respect it, nodding slowly.

Andrew continued, "I know you and your daughter have been estranged, but we'd like to see if we can change that."

Layla wasn't sure she liked the way Andrew had taken over, but it seemed to make her father relax more.

"I'm assuming you're romantically involved?"

Andrew nodded. "Yes sir. And I believe in respecting the family when it comes to things like this."

Layla's father gave him a respectful nod. Layla had yearned for that look most of her life. How had Andrew gotten it so easily?

"You're not Mexican?"

Andrew tensed beside her. He probably hadn't been expecting such an overt question, but it didn't surprise Layla at all. Her father was probably extremely happy that Andrew, with his blue eyes, fair skin and hair too light to be anything but Caucasian, wasn't Mexican.

"Does it matter?" Andrew gave her father a challenging look, and she half expected him to claim to be Mexican just because she knew how deeply he cared for her.

Her father shrugged. "I suppose not. Layla's made her own decisions, why should this be any different?"

"I'm not Mexican," Andrew said. "But our children will be."

Layla stilled. They hadn't exactly discussed children, considering Andrew was barely willing to discuss their future as a couple. Yet here he was, talking to her father like they were more serious than she'd thought. For Andrew to be so bold, so decisive . . . whatever else happened, she would never forget the depth of his defense of her. Her dad, however, gave a knowing look as he stood near the doorway.

"So that's what this is about? You're pregnant, aren't you? How much money do you want?"

Pregnant. Clearly her father knew nothing about her, and the thought of how he'd so readily misjudged her made her feel sick.

"No! I've never asked you for money. Do I look pregnant?" Layla started to stand, but Andrew held her back.

"We're not after your money," Andrew said.

Having it confirmed that they weren't interested in his money seemed to mollify her father, though he still stood like he was on guard.

Layla's stomach churned. She might not be pregnant, but she felt like she was going to be sick. Did her father know her at all? At least it confirmed her belief that they were too different for things to work out between them.

Andrew patted Layla's hand again. "My relationship with your daughter has been nothing but honorable, and I intend to do things the right way. Which is why we came here. I thought that if we made an honest effort at reconciliation, Layla and I could move forward with our lives with the whole family. She's not pregnant, but, I hope she will be some day. And it would be nice for those future children to know their grandfather."

Then Andrew shook his head. "But I'm getting ahead of myself. We're just dating. I haven't asked her to marry me because I wanted her father's permission first. Maybe that sounds old-fashioned, but I respect traditions, and I respect family. I want the union of our families to be as complete as possible."

Layla tried not to tear up at his words. Maybe they hadn't specifically discussed their relationship, but Andrew had told her of his plans to get a counseling degree and had asked her opinion on them, even going so far as to discuss schooling options with her.

Her father seemed to take in Andrew's words, looking at him, then at Layla.

"You said you came from Idaho?"

Andrew nodded. "Our family farm is near where Layla's mother grew up. The Quintanas are good friends of mine, but I know there is a hole in Layla's heart where her father is missing."

"Bigby, you said? I seem to remember meeting some Bigbys when I was in Idaho a long time ago."

Which basically meant he'd lied when he'd told her all those years ago that he had no idea where her mother's family was from.

"Typical Mexicans," he'd said. "Never putting down roots for long."

She'd believed him when he said he'd heard they'd all moved to someplace in California. But most of them had never left Arcadia Valley. Where her father had once been.

Her stomach ached at the revelation. She'd spent years trying to track down her mother's family, working for home health companies that paid terrible wages but gave her the freedom to search for her family. And the flexibility to move from town to town when leads dried up. If it hadn't been for seeing Alex Quintana the baseball player on television in a restaurant one night, she might have still been looking. But he'd resembled a picture of her grandfather when her grandfather was young, so Layla decided to find out where Quintana was from and track him down. As it turned out, he was her cousin.

Neither man seemed aware of the depths of betrayal she felt over this new information, but as Andrew squeezed her hand again, Layla knew he supported her.

"Then you've met my family," Andrew said. "We're the only Bigbys around."

"The ones I met seemed to be good people," he said. "I haven't been there in years."

Her father's pleasant tone made her sick. All the times she'd asked, he'd known, and lied.

"You're welcome to come any time. We'll be more than happy to have you."

The apartment door opened, and a woman walked in. She was of medium height, and with her bleach-blonde hair and slender figure, she was the furthest thing from Layla's mother.

"Ed, I didn't know we had visitors. You should have told me. I would been home sooner."

The woman had a pleasant, well-modulated voice like she'd gone to boarding school or some other fancy place. Now that this woman was here, the apartment made perfect sense.

"Cynthia, darling." Her father stood and greeted the woman with a hug and a kiss. Then he turned and gestured at Layla and Andrew. "I didn't know we were having visitors. This is," he gave a very long pause that made Layla wonder if his wife even knew about her.

Layla stood. "I'm Layla. His daughter."

The surprise on Cynthia's face made Layla feel even more like they shouldn't have come. But then, something extraordinary happened. Cynthia crossed the room and put her arms around her.

"Layla! You have no idea how long I've waited for this." Cynthia hugged her tight, like she was a long-lost friend.

"You know who I am?"

Feeling stiff in this strange woman's arms, Layla pulled away. Cynthia seemed so unlike anyone she could picture in her father's life.

"Of course. Your father has told me a great deal about you. But he is so stubborn, and even though I've tried to get him to contact you, his pride hasn't let him."

Andrew stood and held his hand out to Cynthia. "I'm Andrew. I came here with Layla to help her reestablish her relationship with her father. Pride keeps a lot of us from happiness. Hopefully we can all move beyond it to a brighter future."

"I like you already," Cynthia said, smiling at Layla's father. "You see, Ed, I just knew our prayers would work."

She turned to Layla and winked. "Of course, I prayed that he would stop being so stubborn, so having you come visit is even better. Don't you just love how God gives so lavishly?"

Layla still couldn't wrap her brain around the situation. She'd known that her father preferred the American version of his first name, but she'd never heard him called it. Her mother had said it was so boring.

She'd been fighting her father for so many years, trying to get him to accept her, but had she accepted him?

Wasn't acceptance what they all wanted?

"God has been working in my heart for sure," Layla said, smiling. "Please, tell me about yourself, and how you ended up with my father."

Her father looked uncomfortable, then Cynthia launched into a tale of how Layla's father had worked for her father's company, and how they'd met by chance when Cynthia had gone to visit her father.

"My father and I had been fighting," Cynthia said with a sigh. "He wanted me to come back to work for him, and I just hate the corporate world. I wanted to be an artist and do something that would inspire people."

Cynthia cast a loving glance over at Layla's father. "But Ed told me about how much he missed his own daughter, and how he'd do anything to change the way you two parted. I realized I couldn't lose my family, so I went and apologized to my father, since I knew he would never apologize to me. And my life has never been the same. Ed and I are on the Board of Directors for NarCorp, and we're partnering with some amazing people to hopefully put man back on the moon."

Layla tried not to gag. Basically, her father had advised Cynthia to do the opposite of what was happening here. Give in. Which is what he thought Layla was doing now. Cynthia might think he missed her, but he'd never done anything to make her think he cared about her.

"That sounds wonderful, Cynthia, I'm so glad you found your passion. And my father. I'm happy for you both."

Her father cleared his throat. "You can see why I'd be so hesitant at first. NarCorp is a large corporation, and many people come looking to us with dollar signs in their eyes. It seemed strange to hear from you out of the blue after all these years."

"God," Cynthia said, nudging him. Then she turned to Layla and smiled. "I have been praying, ever since I heard your father's story, that God would reunite you and repair your relationship. I'm so glad your rebellion is over."

Her rebellion?

"I'm not sure what you mean," Layla said, trying to sound pleasant.

Andrew's hand on her leg increased its pressure, so she knew she'd done so-just barely.

"When you ran away from home, of course. What a terrible thing for a father to go through, having his only child run away and not tell him where she went."

At least now she knew the narrative that had snagged Cynthia.

"He knew where I went," Layla said. "I told him I was going to find my Mexican relatives and get to know them."

Even though she didn't want to cause trouble for him and his wife, she couldn't let him get away with the lies that had made her life so hard for so many years.

"Had he simply told me where to find them, it would have been easy for him to contact me. But since he claimed not to know where they were, I spent years searching the country looking for them."

She glared at her father, making sure he understood that she wasn't letting him off the hook for his lies.

Cynthia looked confused. "Ed's not Mexican. He has some Spanish in him, but he's not Mexican. We don't even like Mexicans."

Completely ignoring Andrew's strangled noise, Layla stood. "His full name is Eduardo Ruben Avila Flores. He was born in El Paso, Texas, to a couple of undocumented workers. My mother, Ana Maria Quintana, was born in Arcadia Valley, Idaho, to American citizens of Mexican descent. I didn't run away, I told him I wanted to meet my Mexican family, whom he said left Arcadia Valley years ago. Which they didn't. So I'm sorry if you don't like Mexicans. He's one. And I'm one. God's got a pretty good sense of humor, doesn't He?"

The horror on her father's face was almost worth the humiliation of this experience. Not all family reunions turned out happy.

Cynthia still looked confused as she turned to Layla's father. "But your driver's license says you're Edward Ruben Avery."

"I am," her father said, glaring at Layla. "Do you see the trouble you've caused here with your bizarre Mexican fascination?"

"I am Mexican," Layla said, shaking her head. "But if you need to be an American, go for it."

She remembered the business card her father had given Andrew. They hadn't looked at it, but it obviously would have the name Cynthia used. What had he thought would happen when she called, asking for him?

Then she turned to Cynthia. "I'm very sorry for disrupting your household. But if you're sincere in your wishes for a reconciliation between us, you can find me in Arcadia Valley, Idaho. You'll have to learn to like Mexicans, at least some of us, anyway. I don't know why you don't like Mexicans, but I hope someday you get to know some of us and find we're not so bad."

Looking over at Andrew, who still sat on the couch, Layla said, "Let's go. I tried, it failed. We'll never speak of this again."

When the door closed behind them, Layla wanted to weep. But she kept the tears in check as they got on the elevator and rode it down to the lobby. They'd walked about a block, to the edge of a park, when Layla just couldn't do it anymore.

She collapsed on a bench and started to cry.

Chapter Fifteen

So much for the optimism that everything would work out in Layla's life as easily as it had in his own. Andrew put his arms around her as she sat on a park bench, sobbing.

"His rejection was not about you," Andrew said, holding her tight. "Clearly he rejects his heritage, as evidenced by his name change. I'm sorry that things didn't go nearly as well as we'd hoped."

Layla looked up at him, red-eyed. "He lied to his wife about me. Lied about being Mexican. What kind of marriage is built on lies?"

"Not ours." Andrew kissed the top of her head. "I really thought today would go differently. We would meet your father, he'd turn out not to be such a jerk, and I'd pull him aside, ask him if I could marry you, and then tonight, I was going to take you to one of my favorite places to walk, a place I hadn't taken Mykel, and ask you to marry me."

The look she gave him made him regret his words. Like he'd said the wrong thing at the wrong time.

"Did I do the Mr. Darcy thing again? I was just trying to

make you feel better because I completely messed this up." Andrew ran a hand over his face. "All right. When we get home, I'll take Allie's advice and I'll sit down with all those movies she said I need to watch to learn about women, and-"

Layla pulled him to her and kissed him.

Was it wrong to thoroughly enjoy the kiss of a crying woman? To love the feel of her in his arms? To know that even though he'd ruined everything, she still wanted to kiss him?

As Andrew deepened the kiss, he decided that if that was the case, he didn't want to be right.

Someone in the distance whistled, and Andrew realized that they weren't in a great place to be kissing.

"Sorry about that," he said, pulling away. "I got carried away."

Layla smiled at him, tears still in her eyes, but a peaceful expression on her face. "Me too. But it felt good, and I have no complaints. However, I would just like to have on record that I'm not the only person in this relationship who likes to fix things."

He couldn't help laughing. He'd definitely done his share of trying to fix Layla. "I'm sorry that I encouraged you to seek him out."

"Don't be." She let out a long breath. "I think you were right. I needed the closure. And I needed your perspective, that he's not rejecting me. He's rejecting being a Mexican. Edward Avery? If that's who he wants to be, then fine. But I get to be me."

Andrew couldn't help giving her another quick kiss. "And being you is why I love you so much. You embrace who you are and don't apologize for that."

The smile that lit her face made him wonder how he could have fought her love for so long.

"I know you're afraid that with all the changes you're making in your life, that I'm going to love you less," Layla said. "But the truth is, the more I see your strength in facing your insecurities and fears, the more I love you. No matter what you do, or what direction you go in, I'll be with you every step of the way."

He pulled her close to him once more, but instead of kissing her, he held her tight, listening to the sound of her heart. Somewhere in that space was a depth of love he couldn't have imagined possible.

"I'm with you, too," Andrew said, finally moving so he could look up at her. "Now that you're getting settled in Arcadia Valley with your family, I don't know what your ambitions are for your life. But whatever they are, I want to support you."

She looked at him coyly. "Well, you mentioned something about children at my father's place . . ."

Andrew had forgotten about his spur of the moment declaration. He'd been so angry at her father's pleasure that he wasn't Mexican that he'd let his emotions take over.

"I'm sorry, that was presumptuous of me, talking about children when we hadn't discussed it."

Layla put her arms around him again. "Oh, I want children. Lots of children. Enough for a soccer team, or a baseball team, or a football team, whatever kind of team has lots of players. I'm not really into sports, but I like the idea of having enough kids to take over a small country."

He couldn't tell whether or not she was joking, so he mulled the idea in his head. He'd thought maybe a couple of kids, but could he handle more?

"I'm kidding," Layla said, giving him a small kiss. "How would we fit all those children in that tiny house of yours?"

He hadn't even thought about living arrangements. Layla's apartment was bigger than his tiny house. Would she be willing to move to someplace so small? Or would they need to figure out a new place to live? Hopefully not somewhere too far from the farm. Could he build something on the farm?

"Hey!" Layla waved her hand in front of him. "Stop trying to figure out how you're going to pay for all those diapers. You haven't asked me to marry you yet, and I haven't said I would."

He couldn't help laughing, and Layla quickly joined in.

Then he looked around the park where they sat, not even fully sure where they were.

"Do you need something romantic and planned out, or will this do?"

She appeared to consider his question. Then she shrugged. "I'm starting to think that the plans we make are the furthest from the plans God has for us. So whatever God puts on your heart, that's what I want from you."

What was God telling him? Probably that he'd be a fool to go a minute longer without making Layla a more permanent fixture in his life.

Andrew shifted his weight so he was down on one knee. He reached into his pants pocket, glad that he'd already put the ring there for the proposal he'd originally prepared.

"Layla, what God has put on my heart is that I'd be crazy not to spend my life with you. You've made me a better man, and until you came along, the thought of romance made me sick. But now, all I want is for you to be my wife. I may not be Mexican, but I promise you, our kids will be. Will you marry me?"

Once again, she wrapped her arms around him. "I thought you'd never ask."

She kissed him, then pulled away for a moment and stared at him. "Literally. I thought you would never ask."

A contented expression filled her face. "But I am so glad you did, because nothing would make me happier than to be your wife."

As Andrew slid the ring onto her finger, Layla stared at it. She'd know the diamond surrounded by a bunch of tiny diamonds to look like a flower anywhere. "This is Enid's ring."

He nodded. "She cornered me as I was leaving to pick you up to come here. She pulled it off her finger and handed it to me, telling me that if I didn't propose, I was an idiot."

Layla laughed. "So you asked me to marry you to avoid your grandmother's wrath?"

"No. I pulled out the ring I'd bought at Facets and told her I was planning on it. She said the one I'd chosen was a worthless piece of junk, and if I wanted a happy marriage I'd give you her ring, which my grandfather gave her, which his grandmother had given him. We Bigbys don't have much, but this represents over a hundred years of Bigby commitment, and that's what I'm offering you."

His eyes misted as he thought of all the Bigby brides who'd worn this ring. Especially as he saw it twinkling on Layla's finger. Gram had been right. Compared to this, the ring he'd chosen had been junk.

Layla started to cry. "All my life, I wanted to be part of a big family, full of love and tradition. I'd hoped to find it when I came to Arcadia Valley to meet my Quintana relatives, but now I know my family isn't complete without yours. I'm honored to wear the Bigby ring, and your grandmother is right, anything else would be junk."

They kissed, and as Andrew held Layla for the first time as his fiancée, his heart swelled as he realized the truth of what Pastor Harris and Ben had told him. His ability to love was limitless, and would only grow as he and Layla shared their lives.

Epilogue

Layla tore open the pretty stationery without a return address. Probably another flyer from a bridal shop. But considering Andrew had agreed to a Mexican wedding, and she was still on the hunt for the perfect dress to express her heritage, she'd read any and all ads if they helped.

"What's that?" Andrew came around the corner, using a rag to wipe his hands dirtied from yet another attempt at getting his stupid tractor to run. The family was all starting to lean towards going out and buying a new one, but he still stubbornly refused, saying he'd get it running yet.

"I don't know. I haven't looked at it." As she pulled the contents of the envelope out, she realized it was a letter.

From Cynthia.

She scanned the letter, then let it flutter to the ground.

"What does it say?" Andrew reached for it.

Tears rolled down Layla's face. "Cynthia wants to know if they can come for a visit. My father isn't ready to see the Quintanas, but he understands he was too hasty in dismissing me."

As he scanned the document, his brow furrowed. "She wrote it, not him. But she sounds very sincere."

"She was," her father's voice came from the other side of the yard. He came closer, carrying a box.

"I decided to take my chances and just show up because after how I treated you, you would have every right to tear up Cynthia's letter and throw it away. We fought for a long time after you left. She called me out on a lot of things, and she was right."

He held the box out to her. "I imagine that you two are planning a wedding. The way Andrew looked at me, and the way he looked at you, I could tell he loves you. Enough that I thought he might kill me for how I'd treated you."

Andrew stepped forward. "She deserves better."

"She does." Her father closed his eyes, like he was trying to find the strength to continue. Then he looked at Layla. "I hated being a Mexican. Going to school, the kids called me names and bullied me. As an adult, people treated me differently, like I wasn't worthy of respect. When you left, I decided to be the man I wished I could have been had I not been Mexican."

Layla's heart hurt for him, but also for herself because she remembered Andrew surmising that was the case. She'd been hard on him, but she hadn't known he'd faced such bullying.

"I wasn't any happier," he finally said. "But I fooled myself into thinking so. I kept a few of your mother's things. I couldn't get rid of them, but I didn't know what to do with them. So, here. I hope they will make you happy."

Layla took the box and opened it. The pictures she remembered in her home growing up sat on top, mementos from her mother's childhood. She even recognized a few old photos of Arcadia Valley.

"Look at these!" She handed the pictures to Andrew then turned to her father. "Thank you. This gift means a lot."

He shifted uncomfortably. "Your mother's wedding dress is in there. It probably needs some work, and it's probably out of style, but I know sometimes women like things like that."

Layla tore through the box, then pulled out a bunch of yellowed fabric. Holding it up to the light, she could see that it did, in fact, need a lot of work. But as she remembered admiring her mother's wedding picture as a child, she knew she'd do what it took to make the dress work for her own wedding.

She stood then reached out to her father, giving him a hug. "Thank you. You don't know how perfect this is."

He returned the hug awkwardly. "You're welcome. I don't know why I didn't give it to you sooner."

Layla looked around. "Where's Cynthia? I'm sure she had a role in this. I'd like to thank her as well."

"She's with her parents." Her father looked nervous. "She, uh, found out she was pregnant shortly after you visited us. And um, she doesn't want me ruining another child's life. We're seeing, um . . ."

Andrew nodded encouragingly. "If you're seeing a counselor, there's nothing to be ashamed of. Layla and I are doing premarital counseling, and I'm studying to be a counselor. We all need help from time to time."

Putting her arm around Andrew, Layla smiled. They'd worked through a lot of their issues already, but she appreciated how he still looked to improve things between them.

"I didn't think Cynthia believed me when I told her I regretted my actions with you. I thought if I just came to see you, she would know that I meant it."

He looked like he was about to cry, and Layla almost felt sorry for him, except part of her wondered if he was just there because he hoped to win Cynthia back.

"She's right," he said slowly, his voice sounding choked. "I wasted a lot of time pushing you away and trying to make you fit into a mold where you didn't belong. I have a lot of things to work on, and I need to learn how to be a better man in time for this baby to be born. I don't want to do to him or her what I did to you. I'm sorry. I thought I was protecting you from being hurt, only I did the opposite."

Layla hugged him again, holding him tight. "I forgive you. I was also unreasonable at times, and I didn't try to see things from your perspective. But my relationship with Andrew taught me that the test of real love is about how well you're able to forgive and move on. So let's see if we can make that work, okay?"

Her father pulled away and nodded, then looked over at Andrew. "Thank you for loving my daughter so well."

"It's only because she loved me first. I know you didn't come here to get an invitation." Andrew looked over at Layla as if asking for permission.

She nodded, then came back to stand next to him and took his hand. Layla had given up on the idea of having her father part of their wedding. But the warmth in her heart made her grateful Andrew never had.

Squeezing Layla's hand, Andrew said, "I hope that you'd be

willing to be part of our wedding and will walk Layla down the aisle."

Whatever had been keeping her father from crying stopped working. He began to sob openly. "I didn't know how much that would mean to me until just now. Thank you. I'm so sorry for everything I've done."

Layla hugged him again. "I know. So now we do better. Go home to Cynthia, and help her get ready for my new brother or sister. And we'll keep you posted on the wedding arrangements."

This time, her father hugged her tight, and Layla couldn't believe how loved she felt in his arms. They still had a long way to go, but she knew it would be all right.

The sound of an engine in the distance made Layla jump.

"Hey," Andrew said. "That's my tractor!"

They all ran over to the tractor, where Enid was tinkering with something underneath while McKenna sat in the cab.

"What are you doing?" Andrew ran up to them, and Enid slid out and held out her hand.

"I need a rag for all this grease. I remembered that the grannies and I rigged up part of the engine to get it to go faster for the tractor races, only we made it blow. I forgot to tell you what we'd done, and since I just remembered, I thought I'd fix the part we broke."

Enid looked absolutely unrepentant. In fact, she seemed almost gleeful.

"All this time, you knew what was wrong with my tractor?"

The old woman shrugged. "I did, but I forgot that I knew. I think at first I was afraid you'd be mad since we were the ones who broke it. Then I just forgot. But it's fixed now, so you can plow over all those cucumbers I thought I wanted. The folks from Corinna's Cupboard took all the fruit, so now we can use the space for something else instead."

Turning to Layla, Enid said, "How do you feel about rutabagas?"

"No, Gram, no."

As Andrew argued with his grandmother, Layla turned back to her father.

"You see? Families fight sometimes, and it's hard. But in a little while, Andrew will be running around, gladly doing some weird thing Enid asked him to do. Because he loves her. And in the end, love is stronger than any conflict, if we let it rule in our lives."

Arcadia Valley Romance: Six authors. Six series. One community.

Welcome to Arcadia Valley, Idaho, where a foodie culture and romance grow hand-in-hand. Join my friends and me as we release a book every month set in Arcadia Valley. You'll enjoy meeting old friends and making new ones as each of the six authors' books intertwine with the previous stories in this Christian romance series. Get started with *Romance Grows in Arcadia Valley* and follow along at ArcadiaValleyRomance.com to make sure you don't miss any installments!

AN

Arcadia Valley

ROMANCE

www.ArcadiaValleyRomance.com

Coming Next in Arcadia Valley

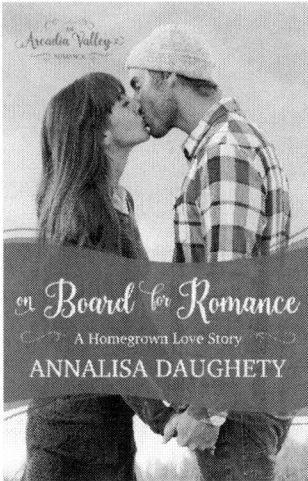

Riley Jennings has spent most of her life rescuing and caring for animals. From her work with a dog rescue organization to her newly opened pet boarding business, she's focused on animals the majority of the time. Even her weekends are spent at the Arcadia Valley Farmers Market selling her homemade dog biscuits and educating the public about fostering and adopting dogs in need. Riley keeps herself so busy she has little time for anything else—especially dating. Her sisters claim she's hiding behind her work so she won't have time for a social life. Chronically introverted Riley much prefers a quiet night at home with her animals than making awkward small talk on a first date. But when a handsome newcomer arrives to town and needs help establishing a pet therapy program, she can't help but be drawn to him.

Blake Taylor came to Arcadia Valley for a fresh start after a troubled past. He's found a dream job at the local nursing home where his beloved grandfather is a resident. When he meets Riley, he's excited about the future for the first time in a long time. But when his past follows him to town, his hope for a fresh start is crushed and Blake worries his new life is over before it even began.

Can Riley let her guard down long enough to get to know Blake? And will Blake ever be able to leave the past behind? If they can learn to trust each other, they may find that there's a better plan in store than either of them ever could have imagined.

On Board for Romance
by Annalisa Daughety

Chapter One

Riley Jennings shifted the large Tabby cat in her arms and tried to stay calm. "Dottie is wearing her rabies tag. The phone number to the vet's office is on there."

The receptionist at Retro Village raised an eyebrow. "I've already explained to you. We need the visiting animal's shot records on file."

"But I don't have the records. She's Mr. Farley's cat and he can't remember what he did with them. I'll go to the vet's office tomorrow and get them, but they're closed today." Mr. Farley had left her a voice mail this morning while she was at church. He'd been so forlorn and was missing his cat so much, she'd rushed home to pick up Dottie and take her to the senior living facility. "Please."

The woman shook her head. "I didn't make the rule, but I also won't bend it."

Dottie meowed loudly as if in protest and Riley scratched

behind her left ear. "It's okay, girl," she murmured. "I know you're not happy." Dottie had been Mr. Farley's most loyal companion since she was just a kitten. She was nearly sixteen now.

"So there's nothing that you can do?" Riley asked. "Can you at least call Mr. Farley and let him know we're here? He can come outside."

The receptionist frowned. "Hold on." She picked up the phone and punched a number.

Riley glanced around. Did the fact that she was contemplating putting Dottie in her oversize bag and sneaking her past reception make her a terrible person? Before she could decide, the receptionist cleared her throat.

"Mr. Farley is ill. He has a slight fever and the head nurse doesn't want him to go outside."

That made it even worse. That sweet elderly man was sick and without the comfort of his cat. Riley was normally slow to anger, but the situation got the better of her. "Fine. But you haven't heard the last of me today." Before the woman could respond, Riley cuddled Dottie to her chest and stormed to her truck.

The blue sky and cotton ball clouds did little to brighten her mood. Late June in Arcadia Valley was lovely, and Riley was normally one to stop and take note, but today she only felt sad for Mr. Farley. He deserved better, and since he didn't have any family around, it looked like it was up to her to make sure he was taken care of.

Thanks to all her work with the animal shelter, not to mention her own pet boarding business, she had the local veterinarian's number in her phone. His home number. "Dr. Wilson?" she asked when he picked up. "You don't happen to have anyone working up at the clinic right now do you? It's Riley Jennings."

Dr. Wilson chuckled on the other end. "Riley, of course I recognize you. Did someone drop a pregnant stray on your doorstep again?" Pregnant strays tied to the porch were a common occurrence at Riley's house. She had lost count of how many she'd taken in. Her track record for successfully finding foster or permanent homes for the abandoned animals of Arcadia Valley was pretty good, too.

She smiled in spite of herself. "Not this time, Doc. Actually I just need the shot records for Mr. Wilbur Farley's cat, Dottie. She can't visit him without them."

"Ah, yes. Mr. Farley and Dottie have been inseparable for years. I'm sure this transition is hard for both of them. Donna is at the clinic now checking on some of our weekend boarders. If you'll go to the back door, it should be unlocked and she can get you a copy of Dottie's records. I'll call her and let her know you are on the way."

"You have no idea how much this means to me. I'll drop a big bag of treats off for your customers to enjoy soon." In addition to dog and cat boarding, Riley also sold homemade treats at the local farmers market.

"You know you don't have to do that, but I also won't turn you down. Everyone loves those treats."

Riley hung up, grinning. *Take that, Miss Follow the Rules Receptionist.*

Twenty minutes later, she and Dottie were back at the desk,

papers in hand. "Here you go. Everything should be in order." Riley smiled and placed the shot record on the counter. "Now can we please go see Mr. Farley?" She couldn't wait to reunite the old man with his beloved cat.

The receptionist typed something into her computer. "Oops." She grimaced.

What now? "What's wrong?"

The woman sighed. "I didn't see this earlier, but unfortunately I'm not going to be able to let you go back to Mr. Farley's room, even with the paperwork in order."

Riley frowned. "I don't get it. I just jumped through a pretty major hoop to get shot records for Dottie so you would have them on file. I had to call in a favor at the vet's office to get that taken care of on a Sunday afternoon. So what exactly is the problem now?" Her voice was sharper than normal, but she didn't care.

"It seems that Mr. Farley has a new roommate. And he's allergic to cats."

"Why in the world would you have put someone with a cat allergy in Mr. Farley's room?" Riley asked. "I know good and well that he indicated on his paperwork that he'd have Dottie visiting. Besides. I thought you only had private rooms." Mr. Farley was frail, but his mind was sharp. He'd brought Dottie to her several weeks ago and opened up about his worries. His main concern was that Dottie wouldn't be treated well. Riley had assured him that if she couldn't find the perfect home for the cat, she would keep her as her own. Either way, she'd promised Mr. Farley that Dottie would visit as much as possible.

The receptionist shrugged. "I'm sorry. There was a bed

availability issue and the way I understand it, Mr. Farley was consulted before a roommate was brought in."

Riley bit her lip and contemplated her options. "Look, ma'am. I understand that there are rules and that you are only doing your job, but I had multiple messages from Mr. Farley today specifically requesting that I bring Dottie to see him. I would be glad to go put Dottie in the car and go get Mr. Farley myself."

The woman looked at her with disdain. "I've already told you. The head nurse—"

Riley cut her off by holding up a hand. "I know. But don't you think that sometimes the love and companionship of a pet can be good medicine for someone not feeling well?"

They regarded each other for a long moment and Riley was sure she'd won the battle.

"No." The woman shook her head. "Come back tomorrow."

"I want to speak to your supervisor." If her sisters could see her now, they'd freak out. Assertiveness wasn't exactly one of Riley's primary traits. But her passion for animals took over sometimes.

The receptionist glared. "It won't do you any good."

"I'd like to try anyway."

The woman dramatically pushed away from her desk and stomped toward a closed door behind the reception area.

Riley glanced down the hallway and then back to the empty reception desk, considering her options.

"I wouldn't do that if I were you," an amused male voice said from behind her. "I'm pretty sure she'll put the whole place on lockdown if she comes back and you aren't still standing here."

Riley turned slowly toward the voice, her cheeks flaming, and found herself staring into the most gorgeous amber eyes she'd ever seen.

**

Blake Taylor hadn't come back to Arcadia Valley after all these years to get distracted by a beautiful woman. But after observing the exchange between the tall, cat-wielding brunette and the scowling receptionist, he couldn't help himself. "I'm just saying. . .I don't think she'd take too kindly to you breaking all the rules and taking that cat down the hallway." He grinned. "Not that I'm all that fond of rules, but in this case it might be in your best interest. I'd hate to see you be the headline on tonight's local news."

The girl gave him a small grin. "I'm a by the book kind of person, but not when it means keeping a sick elderly man and his sixteen year old cat from seeing each other."

"That does sound like a worthy cause." He furrowed his brow. "I've gotten the feeling this place is pet friendly though, so what's the problem?"

She filled him in on things. "I hate to be pushy, but he's called me more than once today, so I know it would mean so much to him."

"Maybe he just forgot he already called," Blake said helpfully. "I mean, he could be a forgetful old man. In fact, maybe he won't even remember he called and asked about the cat in the first place."

The look on her face told him she hadn't considered his words helpful in the least. "I think he will keep calling until he

THE THOUGHT OF ROMANCE

gets to see Dottie." She frowned at him.

"Fair enough." He was eager to change the subject. "I'm Blake, by the way. Blake Taylor."

"Riley Jennings." She eyed him suspiciously. "Do you work here?"

He shook his head. "No. I just rolled into town actually. Visiting a relative." He didn't offer more information than necessary because honestly, he was having a hard time wrapping his head around being back in Arcadia Valley. He was sure he couldn't explain his return to a pretty stranger without coming across sounding like a total idiot.

Riley didn't press him. "I see." She stroked the cat.

"So are you, like, this guy's granddaughter or niece or something? It's pretty nice of you to fight so hard to reunite him with his cat."

That garnered a smile, albeit a small one. "No relation. I have a business boarding animals and I also volunteer for the local animal shelter. Mr. Farley has asked me to re-home Dottie, but he wants to see her as much as possible."

"Can't blame him for that. Pets are family as far as I'm concerned."

Riley's blue eyes twinkled. "Me, too."

Finally. He was getting somewhere. "Where is his room located?"

She pointed to a door to the left side of the reception area. "The place is set up so there are three pods through that door. Each pod contains resident rooms and they share a common area. There's another door to the right of reception that houses three more pods. I'm not sure how many rooms each one contains, but Mr. Farley is in the one on the left side and then go to the far left."

"Does his room look out at anything?"

She nodded. "You can see part of the parking lot from his room. There's a bench right near the sidewalk that you can see from his room as well. I noticed it when I was here last week."

Blake scratched his three-day old stubble. As soon as he found a place to stay tonight, a shower was in order. And a shave. "Well I'm pretty sure we're going to run into trouble when the receptionist gets back. How about I help you?"

"Help me? Are you going to stand guard while I'm in the room?" she asked.

He chuckled. "Nothing like that. In fact, we won't even have to break the rules. Bend them maybe, but not break." He held out his hands. "Give Dottie to me."

She took a step back and put a protective arm over the cat. "Why?"

Blake raised his eyebrows. "Do I really look like someone who is going to steal a sixteen-year-old very overweight cat?"

Riley grinned. "Guess not." She handed the cat over.

Dottie was even heavier than she looked. "You go to the room and get the old man to the window. I'll do the rest."

**

Riley cast a backward glance at Blake as he carried Dottie out the front door. What an unusual day this was turning out to be.

"Miss!" The receptionist yelled down the hall.

Riley whipped around and held her hands up. "I don't have the cat. It's just me and I'm only going to check on Mr. Farley."

Mostly.

The woman regarded her suspiciously for a moment. "Well, okay." With one more wary glance in Riley's direction, she sat back down at the desk.

Riley hurried down the hallway toward Mr. Farley's room. She knocked softly on the door.

"Come in," Mr. Farley called.

She pushed the door open and stepped inside.

Mr. Farley sat up in his bed. "I'm so glad to see you, Riley." He looked eager. "Is Dottie here? Is she okay?"

Riley nodded. "She's doing great."

"Have you found her a home yet?" he asked. He furrowed his brow. "She's really a great cat. Make sure the new owner knows how much she enjoys just a little bit of whipped cream." He grinned. "I like a little whipped cream in my coffee, always have. Dottie swiped some once and was hooked ever since."

Riley smiled. "I'll keep that in mind. For now, she is settling in at my place just fine"

He reached out and took her hand as she reached his bedside. "I can't tell you how much that eases my mind. Everyone in town knows how much you love animals. I know you will see to it that my Dottie is cared for properly. She's the only family I have left," he said sadly

Riley patted his arm. "I will take good care of her."

"Where is she?"

"We have a little problem here, Mr. Farley. It seems that your new roommate is allergic to cats," she said as she gestured toward the man sitting in a recliner in the corner.

"Where are my manners?" Mr. Farley asked. "I should have

introduced you to my roommate. This is Charles Thompson."

Riley smiled at the gray haired man. "Nice to meet you, Mr. Thompson. I hope I'm not bothering you by stopping in."

Mr. Thompson nodded. "We don't get to see girls as pretty as you too often." He gave her a wink. "It's nice to have a visitor. And you can call me Charles."

"He just moved in last week, so I guess you can say he's the new kid on the block." Mr. Farley gestured toward his roommate. "We've known one another for several years though, so at least they didn't put me with a stranger."

"That's nice that the two of you know one another."

"But I'm not staying too long," Charles said. "I'm only here to recover from a fall." He frowned. "Not that I don't enjoy Wilbur's company, but I'd just as soon be at home."

Mr. Farley let out a harrumph. "Wouldn't we all?" He picked up the framed photo of Dottie sitting on his nightstand. "I miss my Dottie and my favorite coffee mug. And my old easy chair."

"Getting old is for the birds," Charles agreed. "But I've convinced my son to let me try to make it at home for a while longer once my hip is fully healed and I've completed the torture—I mean rehab—they make me do." His eyes twinkled. "I still have a few things I want to take care of before I spend the rest of my days beating Wilbur at checkers."

Mr. Farley rolled his eyes. "You wish. And torture my foot. They only make him walk a few steps at a time. Why, when I was in the Army—"

Charles snorted. "Army? How about me and my years as a marine? I know a thing or two about physical fitness, too."

Before the discussion went any farther, Riley stepped to the window. She raised the shade and waved to Blake. "There's someone here to see you, Mr. Farley."

"Out the window?" he asked.

"Can you see out there okay?"

Blake pressed his face to the window and his eyes grew wide as he looked around the room.

"What's wrong?" she mouthed.

He shook his head and just as quickly as he'd been there, he was gone.

"Um, hang on." Riley peered outside and watched as Blake waved a kid over from the parking lot. He handed Dottie to the boy and pointed to the window where Riley stood. What was going on?

The boy brought Dottie to the window and held her up to the window sill.

"My Dottie!" Mr. Farley exclaimed. "Help me get up, please."

Riley opened the window. "Thanks," she said to the puzzled pre-teen. "Just hang on a few minutes, please."

"Sure." The kid didn't look put out by Blake's cat handoff.

She helped Mr. Farley to his feet and put his walker within his reach. "Be careful."

He shuffled over to the window. "I'm so happy to see you." He reached through the open window and stroked Dottie's fur.

Riley beamed. These reunions always made her so happy. She left him with Dottie and mouthed a silent 'thank you' to the boy.

"That's a nice thing you did," Charles said. "He's been missing that cat a whole lot." He sighed. "I hate that I'm the reason she can't come in to visit. I'm fine with dogs. Even horses and farm animals don't bother me. But cats have always made me sneeze."

She smiled. "It's not your fault." She stepped over to his side of the room where a handful of family photos sat on his nightstand. "Is this your family?"

He nodded. "Sure is. My wife framed those years ago, and they always sat on our nightstand, even after she passed away. When I left the hospital to come here and stay for rehab, my daughter-in-law brought them and put them up. She said I needed a little touch of home."

"I'm sure she's right." One of the photos caught her eye and she picked it up.

A handsome guy in a tux filled the frame, clearly a senior photo from several years back.

"That's my grandson."

Riley stared at the face. The familiar face. The face of the cute guy who'd just ditched Mr. Farley's cat in the parking lot.

Charles Thompson's grandson was none other than Blake Taylor.

The Arcadia Valley Romance Series

January 2017: *Romance Grows in Arcadia Valley*
February 2017: *Summer's Glory* by Mary Jane Hathaway
March 2017: *Muffins & Moonbeams* by Elizabeth Maddrey
April 2017: *Secrets of the Heart* by Lee Tobin McClain
May 2017: *Sprouts of Love* by Valerie Comer
June 2017: *The Thought of Romance* by Danica Favorite
July 2017: *On Board for Romance* by Annalisa Daughety
August 2017: *Autumn's Majesty* by Mary Jane Hathaway
September 2017: *Cookies & Candlelight* by Elizabeth Maddrey
October 2017: *Wise at Heart* by Lee Tobin McClain
November 2017: *Rooted in Love* by Valerie Comer
December 2017: *The Sound of Romance* by Danica Favorite
January 2018: *A Recipe for Romance* by Annalisa Daughety
February 2018: *Winter's Promises* by Mary Jane Hathaway
March 2018: *Donuts & Daydreams* by Elizabeth Maddrey
April 2018: *Joy of My Heart* by Lee Tobin McClain
May 2018: *Harvest of Love* by Valerie Comer
June 2018: *The Taste of Romance* by Danica Favorite
July 2018: *A Reservation for Romance* by Annalisa Daughety

About the Author

A self-professed crazy chicken lady, Danica Favorite loves the adventure of living a creative life. She and her family recently moved in to their dream home in the mountains above Denver, Colorado. Danica loves to explore the depths of human nature and follow people on the journey to happily ever after. Though the journey is often bumpy, those bumps are what refine imperfect characters as they live the life God created them for. Oops, that just spoiled the ending of all of Danica's stories. Then again, getting there is all the fun.

Subscribe to Danica's newsletter for all her latest news:
http://eepurl.com/7HCXj

You can connect with Danica at the following places:

Amazon: https://www.amazon.com/Danica-Favorite/e/B00KRP0IFU
BookBub: https://www.bookbub.com/authors/danica-favorite
Website: http://www.danicafavorite.com/
Twitter: https://twitter.com/danicafavorite
Instagram: https://instagram.com/danicafavorite/
Facebook: https://www.facebook.com/DanicaFavoriteAuthor

51544915R00138

Made in the USA
Columbia, SC
19 February 2019